THE FACE OF HEAVEN

Borgo Press Books by BRIAN STABLEFORD

THE FACE OF HEAVEN

THE REALMS OF TARTARUS, BOOK ONE

BRIAN STABLEFORD

THE BORGO PRESS

MMXII

THE FACE OF HEAVEN

FIRST BORGO PRESS EDITION

Published by Wildside Press LLC

www.wildsidebooks.com

ACKNOWLEDGMENTS

I am greatly obliged to Heather Datta for her great kindness and consummate efficiency in scanning the text of the first edition of this novel, thus enabling me to get it back into print.

THE FACE OF HEAVEN

1.

The stars stood still in the sky, as they always had, as they always would. They shone with a steady pearl-white light. Each one was perfectly round. They were not evenly distributed in the sky. They clustered above the land that was called Shairn, and they grew hardly less dense towards the east, where the lands of the Men Without Souls stretched away from Cudal Canal farther than the eye could see from Amalek Height. To the north of Shairn was the Swithering Waste, and in those skies the stars were set farther apart, and farther still as one went west of north, skirting the great wall of iron. Ultimately, in the far west of north, were the blacklands, where no stars shone at all except for a single line which curved away into the darkness: a road of stars. No one followed the road of stars, not because no one was curious as to where it might lead and why, but because the blacklands sheltered creatures which preferred to stay away from the lightlands and from men of all kinds, and the men were afraid of them.

To the west and southwest of Shairn the stars shone brightly enough, but those were bad hills, stained with poison and incurable disease. There were nomad paths—allegedly safe paths—across the hills, but only the Cuchumanates dared use them unless need forced fugitives to take the risk. To the south itself was more good land—the land called Dimoom by the Children of the Voice.

Chemec was crouched on top of the hill called Clauster Ridge, sheltering beneath the umbrella of a sourcap from the light of the stars. Clauster Ridge was by no means the impressive peak that Amalek Height was, but it brought Chemec far too close to the stars for him to feel truly comfortable. He felt that, as he watched the Livider Marches which stood unused between the ridge and Cudal Canal, so the stars kept watch on him. But someone had to keep watch—someone always had to keep watch in these troubled times. Old Man Yami was getting old, and the young Ermold across the canal was aching for a fight and a chance to take a few skulls. For any reason, or for no reason at all.

In fact, with the sourcaps all around him, Chemec could hardly *watch* at all, but he took a liberal interpretation of his duty, and he had every faith in his nose. The fashion these days was to train eyes rather than noses, but Chemec could never really come round to the idea of counting the stars his friends in the great war of life. They were, at best, neutral. Whereas odors....

He was also listening for movements in the fields of asci which carpeted the gentler slope of the ridge behind him. If anything edible went by, he might as well catch it, and he definitely did not want to be caught unawares by one of his own people. The wind—a gentle enough wind—blew direct from Walgo. It always had and it always would.

When he caught the signal, it came sharp upon the wind, like a tiny stab in his sinuses. It was a cold smell, and a weird smell. A smell that was distinctly alien. It came to him with such a shock that he imagined a shadow rushing on him from the east, and he leapt to his feet, swinging his stone axe out of the cradle of his arms and into readiness for attack. But the shadow was nothing.

He moved with a strange sideways shuffle, something like a crab. One of his legs was bent, the bone having been broken when he was very young. He had learned to live with the deformity. He had the reputation of being a lucky man. When he wanted to move quickly he scuttled like a spider, and one could never quite judge his direction while his head was bobbing and his shoulders weaving.

The sharp smell was a liar. Nothing was close at hand. Whatever it was, it was out of sight. But it *was* coming, slowly. Chemec waited, wondering and worrying, ready to stay or run as the event might demand.

Something new, to him, meant something terrible.

2.

The stars stood still in the sky. Pearl-white light. Every star perfectly round, no matter how close his imagination soared, no matter how far it crept, huddling into the mud and the foul earth. Always the same stars. Always still-standing, white-shining. Always.

Carl Magner, sweating in his sleep, dreaming a dream which, for him, was filled with horror and mystery, had no possible idea of what those stars might signify, and why. He only knew that they seemed to be perpetually falling upon him, threatening him and taunting him with a cold, steely anger.

Magner liked stars. Real stars. Stars which shone weakly, pin-point stars which wheeled their way slowly across the night sky and faded in the west when dawn came. He felt an attraction to those stars. They meant something to him—something real and safe and ultimately knowable if, for the time being, unknown.

But while the stars wheeled Magner slept, and his sleep took him into the world of alien stars which acted as stars should not.

They were the stars of Hell.

Carl Magner had no real understanding of his nightmares. There was no one who could help him to understand. Nightmares no longer existed as signs and symptoms and real phenomena. No one—except Carl Magner—had nightmares. The word was a label that had become a lie. There were no nightmares, supposedly. Carl Magner was alone. There was no one to help him, no help to be offered.

In fleeing the fall of the stars, Magner kept company with all manner of strange creatures—creatures whose names were also lie-labels, but whose being might once have been real, or at least hypothetical. He could name them—most of them—but he could not understand them. He had no preconceived attitude appropriate to them, nor any chain of logic which might help him decide.

They were the creatures of Hell. True Hell. Real Hell.

Not Dante's Inferno, but Euchronia's Tartarus. The Underworld. The world beneath the bowels of the Earth.

Knowing as he did that Hell was real, and knowing that there was no conceivable doubt of that fact, Carl Magner had little alternative but to accept the revelations of his dreams as realities. Because dreams were extinct, the unreality of dreams was by no means axiomatic. It did not even seem probable to Carl Magner. He looked upon the experiences of his sleep as an extra sense—an ultra-sight. There was no other way he *could* think of them.

Given that Hell was real, given that the nightmare experience was real, Carl Magner had no alternative but to think that the urgency of the dream, the madness of the dream, the fierceness of the dream, and the fearfulness of the dream were meaningful. The feelings of fear and compulsion were purposeful. Magner thought—and what else could he think?—that the dreams were not only trying to tell him something, but trying to make him act on it. He alone, of the millions of men who inhabited Euchronia's Millennium, was prey to this compulsion, this fear, this need.

There was something messianic in the very fact of his perennial nightmare.

In Magner's dreams, the Underworld was filled—positively *filled*, or it seemed so—with people. People living under the stars, *trapped* forever under the cold light of the alien stars. It was their terror which Magner felt, or so he thought. It was their compulsion.

He hardly sensed the people as individuals at all. He was aware of them *en masse,* as a unit, as a gargantuan hive organism, perpetually growing, and dying by degrees. But it was essentially human. He sensed the people of the Underworld as a whole race, but it was definitely a human race. Magner could identify with those people—he *was* identified with them. In his sympathy, he identified his fear with their fear, his nightmare with their nightmare.

Magner, in his sleep, was enmeshed in a gruesome, gluesome phantasmagoria of images which forced him to react. He could not exempt himself from the sensations of feet in sticky earth, lungs filling with dead, fetid air, gullets sucking up filthy water, any more than he could exempt himself from the terror. In his dreams, he was never clean, because excrement of all kinds was *always* close to him. He sweated constantly. It was hot, and worse than humid. It was glutinous.

Often in his dreams he found himself running—from the falling, staring stars, from the fluttering, screaming (?), night-flying moths, from the multicolored, shinyskinned, click-clicking crabs. But the running was so slow, his limbs so gummed down, his environs so thick and turgid, that he never got anywhere at all. The creatures of the eternal night kept coming. Eternally.

They never caught him, save by degrees.

The worst thing of all—absolutely the worst—was the fact that he passed so easily from the Hell-world of his nightmare to the real world of his waking life. The one faded into the other with a casual smoothness like the changing of images in a holo-receiver. The world of his inner, secret life and the world in which he lived as one of the infinitely privileged of Euchronia's Millennium were not merely close. They overlapped.

At best, they touched. At worst, they were one and the same Earth.

Carl Magner believed, deeply and sincerely—and what else *could* he believe?—that his nightmare was a message and a command. He believed that the people of the Underworld were asking...demanding...his help.

3.

Chemec followed the four aliens along the contour of the hill. Their incredible stink was still filling his nostrils, but he had already become used to it, and it was no longer painful or sickening. It was, in the final analysis, only slightly unpleasant. Its pervasive quality made him feel exposed. He felt that he would not be able to smell a harrowhound at close quarters. This scared him, though he must have known that the smell would send a harrowhound running.

In consequence of his fear, Chemec walked with his ears pricked and his eyes—normally quiet and idle—flicking furiously from side to side. Sometimes he brought both eyes forward at once to focus and give him stereoscopic vision, but that was little enough use in the dim outdoors—he considered it a child's trick, or a device for reading by lamplight.

Superficially, the strangers resembled men. Men Without Souls, chiefly. But their clothing was not man-like, if it really was clothing. They were hairless—bald as eggs. They had bulky packs on their backs and they carried things—not axes, not spears, nor knives, but most definitely the produce of Heaven Above. But there was more to their presence here than a visitation from Heaven Above. They were more alien than that. They wore masks, but not painted man-masks after the fashion of the Ahrima. Small masks, with eye- and nose-pieces. They moved like nothing on Earth, walking high and slow, with no semblance of care or caution.

Their strangeness was frightening to Chemec. He stumbled once and disturbed a flight of ghosts. They fluttered madly up into the air and a big bat swooped out of nowhere to snap one of them into its mouth. The rest clicked softly as they spiralled back into the shelter of the silkenhairs, swaying in mid air as their huge papery wings jockeyed for position.

The aliens saw neither the flight of the ghosts nor the swoop of the bat, although no real man could possibly have remained unaware. Chemec could even smell the incident, despite the scent of the aliens. The panic of the ghosts had oozed from their pores into the night air—a warning to all who lurked nearby. But not the strangers.

A few moments later, the aliens did come to a halt—suddenly—and Chemec's heart seemed to recoil as he thought that they might have known he was following all the time. But he was not *that* old—his heart did not stop, and his body froze into perfect stillness. He might have smelled of fear...just a little. But he was entitled to that, while he was dogging the footsteps of the unknown.

But the strangers had not seen Chemec. Instead they had seen Stalhelm, for the first time, nestling in the valley beyond the hill. They had not realized it was there, despite the fact that the slopes on which they now walked bore the unmistakable signs of human usage. Chemec realized that the aliens were idiots. They were crippled in the senses—lame in the very being.

While he was still, a crab walked from the shadow of a cranebow and crossed his path. It was only a few feet away, and he could have picked it up, ripped away its claws and cracked its shell between his teeth in a matter of seconds. But he let it go. He often did. He thought of himself as Chemec the crab. Bent-legged Chemec, who preferred other meat as a matter of distinction and self-pride.

The strangers moved off again, walking straight toward Stalhelm. The villagers knew by now that an enemy—they had to be presumed enemies—was approaching, and they would also know that Chemec was following. They would be sure that he was doing his job, holding his stone axe ready for action. Twice, or maybe more, Orgond and Yewen had brought up the idea of his being made Star King, but he had always been ready to be tested, and he had always passed the test, bent leg notwithstanding. Even Old Man Yami was something of a friend to him, despite the fact that he was crippled. But there had to be limits on friendship for the Old Man. The only certain thing in life was the fact that the Old Man would one day be the Star King, and the Old Man was ever more ready to submit someone else to the test in his place. Nobody wanted to be starshine when his closest friend was sitting by the fire. Friendship had limits.

The strangers walked all the way to the earthwall as if they expected the gates to be opened before them and the people of the village to come out crying welcome. But the gates remained firm, and half a hundred arrows were already notched to bowstring. The warriors of Stalhelm waited, but they were anxious, and when the smell took over their nostrils they would be keen to kill. The aliens had no chance at all of life. If they had not worn masks....

Yami, brave Yami, testing his own patience and his own courage, because he was full of confidence, let them come to the very threshold of his village.

It was a fine and beautiful gate that opened the way into Stalhelm, sown with the bones of a hundred and fifty men, with every skull set in the wall on the grand curve. Every skull was an honest one—or no man would admit otherwise, if it were not so. (In Walgo, so Chemec and every man in the village firmly believed, they sowed their gate with the bones of their own dead. Even their women. But the men of Walgo had no Souls, by definition, and so—to them—it probably did not matter.)

The strangers muttered among themselves as they stood before the skull-gate. Chemec was astonished to hear that they spoke his own language. Real Ingling. He could understand every word they said.

How, he wondered, could aliens know the language of the Underworld? Even the men of the Underworld could not *all* speak Ingling—not good Ingling, at any rate. The Cuchumanates, for instance, had only a few words, and the harrowhounds had some foul barking-language that was exclusively their own (or so it was said).

Chemec moved closer to the strangers, confident by now that

they were practically deaf and without the sense of smell, and they would not know that he was right behind them unless they turned round. They did not turn, but they did stop talking before he had caught the real thread of what they were saying. The great gate of Stalhelm was opening, just a crack.

Chemec had not expected it. He stopped dead, and waited.

Old Man Yami...brave Yami...came out. Only Camlak, hardly more than a boy, was with him. Yami felt the need to stand a test. Perhaps it was wise, bearing in mind the rumors about Ermold's bloodthirst. It did seem that much time had gone into memory since the last Communion of Souls. Yami was preparing in advance for the inevitable challenges. He was dressed in his Oracle clothes, and he was emptyhanded. (But his boy-son Camlak carried a long steel knife. Heaven-sent tool to carve Heaven-come meat.)

A row of faces gradually filled itself in along the earth-wall, fleshed faces mingling with the ice-white skulls. A few children climbed bodily on to the stockade, greedy for the sight and smell of some Heavenly blood. It was probably the only chance they would ever get.

Yami sat on the ground, and indicated that Camlak should sit beside him. Camlak, who was studying the art of leadership in preparation for the day when he would try to take the Old Man's place, took up his assigned position with alacrity, showing no fear whatsoever.

The bone-woven gate oozed shut behind them.

Chemec crouched, eager to see with what kind of mockery the Old Man was going to taunt the strangers before they were slaughtered.

The strangers squatted in a semicircle, waiting for Yami to speak.

"We have come here from the world above," said one of the strangers, pointing, first at himself and then at the sky, as if he thought that Yami was a fool.

"I know that," said Yami calmly.

"My name is Ryan Magner," said the stranger.

"And what have you brought to give us?" demanded Yami.

"We have come to talk to you," said Ryan. "We want to learn about you."

Yami laughed, sharply at first, and then authoritatively, until the warriors on the wall, and the women behind it, and the children swarming everywhere all took up the note and screamed their derision.

The laughter went on for a long time.

4.

In his dreams Carl Magner was drowning. He was dying, and he knew it. The pressure of....

The pressure was intolerable.

Waking, Carl Magner preserved his fear. He was really afraid. Afraid in reality. Something was very wrong.

He knew the secrets of Hell. He did not know that the stars stood still in the sky beneath his feet in the same way that he knew the stars above his head were distant suns, but nevertheless....

The consequences of the knowledge were by no means equivalent. He knew about the excrement and the hothouse effect and the radioactive waste and the wrecked world of prehistory. One way or another, he knew. Such knowledge was not censored from the learning of the citizens of Euchronia's Millennium, but only from the myths. *The Marriage of Heaven and Hell* was complete and plucked clean out of the closets of his mind. He had drawn some inspiration and a vestige of understanding from a study of Blake, but in the end his need to misread and misinterpret the original and twist it to his own purposes had proved unconquerable. He believed in his own fourfold vision, not in Blake's.

Carl Magner was still afraid.

The pressure was forcing him to....

5.

At the end of the second dark age, when the coldness of imminent exterminability became just a little too much to bear, and the clothes of madness too thin to wear (the second dark age is also known as the age of psychosis) it became clear that the world was irrevocably lost. The surface of the Earth was ruined.

The Euchronian Movement became the only significant form of protest against the extinction of knowledge, culture, civilization and other things which human beings might then have called humanity. The Movement specialized in cold equations—for years it had been quoting cold equations as recruitment propaganda and protest against the continuing furious spoilage of the world. In the end, the cold equations became simultaneous, and combined into a single absolute equation. The world was dying. A new world would have to be built. The Movement put in hand plans to construct a shell which would enclose the entire land surface of the Earth: a gigantic platform upon which a new civilization could be built from first principles.

The idea was ludicrous. The equation, however, was capable of only the one solution. In addition, the idea of starting afresh was both exciting and attractive. Most telling of all, it came to represent hope. The Movement adopted a political attitude of casual optimism and continued to play its figures icy cool. It might take a million years. But things might get easier as time went by. Perhaps five hundred thousand would suffice.

The Plan (The Euchronian Plan) got under way. Earth and Earth's humanity did not possess the technology required to raise the platform, nor could they imagine where they were going to get the necessary power. But they began work anyhow.

Even as a gesture, the project was a worthwhile endeavor, and even as a failure it would be quite some gesture. There was no shortage of manpower placed at the disposal of the Planners. The operation began at a thousand points all over the globe. The Movement gobbled up governments and nations, and took over a dispirited world by bloodless revolution. The whole human race, insofar as it was organized, became Euchronia. The rebels were neither expelled nor hated, but merely ignored, as though they had forfeited their humanity.

Work went on, calmly, implacably. Progress was made. And the end remained quite patently impossible. It was not so much that the project was beyond all human ambition and ability, merely that time was so completely set against them. They had not the time to learn because they had not the time to live. The world could not support their effort. The exhausted world simply could not meet its deadlines.

Sisyr's starship arrived on Earth during the first century of the Plan. It was pure coincidence. Reason (cold equations) said that a technology which could build starships could also build a new world, and so Euchronia asked Sisyr for help. He considered the problem in all its aspects and finally declared that the job could be done and that he would take the responsibility on a contractual basis.

He sent a message back to his own people asking for supplies and for technical assistance. The message took decades to cross the interstellar gulf, the supplies and assistance took centuries. In the meantime, Sisyr and several generations of Euchronians collaborated in revising the Plan, educating the labor force and discovering new potentials in the wasted lands of Earth. There *might*, at this point, have been a hypothetical choice between building the new world and reclaiming the old. If so, the commitment of the human race to Euchronia was such that no choice ever became obvious.

Sisyr and a small army of helpers of his own kind supervised the construction of the platform over the next few thousand years. By the time it had grown to cover the Earth's land surface, most of the aliens had gone back to the distant stars.

Sisyr remained to coordinate the rebuilding of a viable civilization on that surface. He assisted in the modeling of the Earth's new surface, he collaborated on the scheme of land management, and he provided designs for the entire pattern of the maintenance of life. The social system itself was designed by the Movement, but it was designed to fit the world and the environment which had been built largely to Sisyr's specifications.

In return for his services, Sisyr was allowed to make his home on the remade Earth. He remained isolated from the Euchronian community, but pledged to keep its laws. He built himself a palace and retired. Some eight or nine hundred years before the Euchronian Plan, in its final form, came to fruition Sisyr had ceased to take any active part in it. Starships called at Earth three or four times each century, but they called on Sisyr, not the people of Earth. The people of Earth had nothing at all to do with starships once all the necessary aid from the starworlds had been delivered.

Sisyr's contribution to the Plan resulted in its successful completion in a little over eleven thousand years—a short time, comparatively speaking. The Euchronians, of course, claimed the triumph as their own—as, indeed, it was. Theirs had been the vision, theirs the labor, theirs the will. Sisyr had only lent them time which they needed badly.

Sisyr, like the Underworld the Euchronians had left behind, remained known to every citizen. But only as a fact, and an irrelevant fact at that. He had no part in the mythology of the New World.

The Euchronian Millennium was finally declared, and the people became free of their total obligation to the Plan. They were released, to enjoy its fruits, to make what they would of their new life. The Movement did not claim that the society it had designed was Utopian, but it did claim that it had Utopian potential. All that was needed to make perfection was the will of the people. The society was designed to be stable, but not sterile. Euchronia's stability was dynamic stability. Neither perfect happiness nor perfect freedom was immediately on tap, but Euchronia did what it could, and waited—with casual optimism—for the reheated equations of life and death to work themselves out.

The completion of the Plan had demanded—indeed, the

whole philosophy of Euchronia had demanded—that while the Plan was incomplete the people should remain single-minded, working together to the same end. The Movement had helped single-mindedness along somewhat, by devious means which seemed to have excellent results. When the Millennium began, the hegemony of the Movement retained those same devious means in order to assist society in its first, difficult years of freedom and readjustment.

The single most remarkable fact about Euchronia's Millennium, about Euchronia itself and its leaders in particular, was the apparent blindness—willful blindness—exhibited with respect to the wider contexts of existence. They lived in a thin stratum, paying no heed whatsoever to the realms of Tartarus below, nor to the infinite universe above. But they lived in the early years of the Millennium in the heritage of eleven thousand years of narrow-mindedness, in which the only fragment of existence which mattered was that thin stratum. It took time for them even to begin to realize that such tight boundaries could not contain them.

6.

The strangers tried to communicate with the Old Man, but he was not interested in communication. He was not interested in their questions or in their reasons. He was interested primarily in showmanship. The aliens were merely the means to his end.

He exposed himself to them, and they did not kill him. He laughed at them, and they were patently hurt by his laughter. Then he made silence fall, and he began to put his patience on show, knowing that the silent waiting would ultimately hurt the invaders as much as the laughter.

Chemec knew that when the silence had stretched far enough, Yami would have the aliens killed. There was no possible question about that. Chemec saw no other way. Nor did the warriors at the wall. There were some inside who *did* see things another way, who might have wished that the demands upon Yami were not as they were. The readers, undoubtedly, saw the advantages implicit in making friends with the men from Heaven. They would have wished to do just that. But they knew as well as Yami did that life was simply not like that. There were ways of doing things which had been well tried.

Outside the gate the boy Camlak probably had more sympathy with the readers' point of view than he had with his father's. He was studying statecraft carefully, but he was still at the stage when he thought that the Old Man was obeyed because it was simply right that others should obey him. He had no conception of the delicate matters of deciding fitness to rule and make decisions. Decisions came hard to Camlak because his judgment was always crowded with motives and reasons and possibilities. His head would have to be clear of all that before he was allowed to take Yami's place.

The silence which Yami had made grew old, and finally died.

"I am Yami," said the Old Man. They were the only words he spoke. He knew the value of words and the majesty of simplicity.

The strangers had grown visibly uneasy once their initial attempts to kill the silence had faded away into muttering confusion and final bewilderment. When Yami spoke, they relaxed as if some wonderful thing had happened. They smiled beneath their macabre masks. One of them reached forward, his hand open as though he wished to take hold of Yami. The Old Man remained still, and stared the hand away as though he were outfacing a snake.

The alien withdrew his hand. "I'm sorry," he said.

The great gate opened again behind the sitting men. Evidently Yami had been playing a prepared part. The end had been decided before he had stepped out of the gate. The strangers sat, quietly and comfortably, seemingly content, while the young woman Myddal fetched bowls of warm liquid, one by one, and placed one in front of each of the aliens. Eventually, she gave the last bowl to Yami. It obviously contained something different because it was not steaming. The strangers saw this, and even though their minds were crippled they evidently suspected something. But the one who had called himself Ryan Magner sipped from his own bowl and signaled with his hand. The others did the same.

Yami drained his bowl, and watched while his victims did the same. Then he laughed again—not loudly, this time, nor insistently. No one joined in. It was the laugh of a private moment— a gesture of personal satisfaction. The laugh was low, and it bubbled over the Old Man's tongue.

"It's poison, Ryan," said one of the strangers, bitterly. Three of them—all except the leader—knew then that they had been murdered. The leader would not admit it, though he must have *felt* it to be true, by now.

"You bastards," said one of the men, as they all struggled to rise. Only one actually managed to make it to his feet.

As the man stood tall, Chemec raised himself to the full extent of his three feet ten inches and reached up to kill the man. He was careful to smash the spine below the atlas vertebra, so as to preserve the skull unblemished.

7.

Burstone dragged the heavy suitcase along the catwalk to the head of the ladder which descended into the depths of the pit. The steady throb of the great machine filled his ears and blotted out the soft footfalls of the man who was following him.

When he reached the ladder Burstone secured the case to a chain which dangled from a wide axle. He pushed it clear of the catwalk and began to wind the handle on the axle, paying out the chain. The lamps which were arrayed in a long line beside the ladder (for the benefit of the maintenance men who occasionally had to attend the machine) were dim and yellow, and the suitcase soon became a blur in the half-light.

Joth paused to wait for Burstone to finish lowering the case. He was perhaps forty or fifty yards away, and he held himself flat against the body of the machine. He was not quite invisible, but Burstone showed no inclination to look back—he had no reason to think that anyone might follow him down here. Hardly anyone ever came down this low. The machine never went wrong and routine checks were made only twice a year or thereabouts.

Joth was sweating quite heavily. He could feel the heat of the machine through the thin cloth of his shirt, and his own flesh seemed to be very hot, glowing with insistent excitement. He had expected it to be warm down here, but he had not expected anything of the quality of his own reaction. The pressure of his heartbeat sent thin waves of nausea through his body. He could not explain himself.

Burstone was also hot, but he had been through this operation a hundred times before. His reactions to what he was doing and how were qualitatively somewhat different from Joth's, but it was in the integration of his psyche with the physiological symptoms that the real difference lay. Joth was experiencing a mixture of fear and excitement, and to him it was raw sensation. Burstone's mixture of feeling was rather more complex, and he was savoring the delicate blend and balance. To him, this was *good.* This was the fulfilment of a real purpose.

It would have been impossible to hear the soft bump as the suitcase hit bottom, but Burstone knew almost to the inch how much of the chain to let out. He was ready for it to go slack, and he wasted no time. The economy of his motions, the fluid efficiency of the whole enterprise, provided a fair measure of the kick. He heaved himself over the edge of the catwalk, placing his feet comfortably into the metal rungs of the slender ladder, and began to descend comfortably and easily.

Joth moved to the head of the ladder. He gripped the rail of the catwalk hard on either side of the gap, squeezed, and then eased his body forward so that he could peer down into the abyss. It scared him. Height, darkness, uncertainty—all these things were relative strangers to his senses. He had every right and reason to be frightened. He waited for a full minute longer than prudence demanded, gathering his courage and determination, before he followed Burstone into the depths.

He could feel the beating of his heart, and it seemed to be racing ever faster by comparison with the deep, steady beat of the machine. He did not know the purpose of the machine. He took machines for granted. Machines were everywhere, and no one asked how they integrated themselves into the complex web of function which supplied human need in almost every way. Machines were the substance of life itself.

Burstone reached the bottom. He was alone in a tiny pool of light, surrounded by an illimitable darkness. Hiding in the darkness was the machine, and machines parasitic upon it, and machines parasitic upon them. There were pipes and wires and bolts and welds. He knew almost nothing about their outlay or their role. He had never felt the need to explore at this level. This level was dead, with nothing to offer a connoisseur's curiosity. Electronic anatomy and mechanical physiology were not his subjects any more than they were Joth's. What Burstone was interested in was life, and life was a long way below him yet.

With complete assurance, needing no light, Burstone moved away from the foot of the ladder, dragging the suitcase behind him.

By the time Joth reached the foot of the ladder Burstone was long gone. Joth cursed his reluctance to descend and crushed a suddenly flowering urge to retrace his path. The anxiety which had made him cling with such fierce determination to the ladder at every step now held his hands tight, and it took a real effort to make them let go and leave him standing on his own feet. He realized now that he was at the very bottom of the world, and the knowledge that space and the Underworld might be only mere inches beneath his feet made him think that he was in imminent danger, somehow, of falling *through* the floor. He strained his ears, but he could hear nothing. He knew he would have to use his torch.

Even by the dim light of the lampcell set in the side of the machine he could see which way Burstone had gone. There was only one blurred pathway through the thick-layered dust—one worn clean by many journeys, but only one pair of feet. And a suitcase.

Joth switched on his torch. It was a tiny device, with a crystal as small as an eyeball. The beam it shone was pencil-thin. It would have been invisible to the human eye. He set out to follow the path through the dust, hoping that Burstone would have already passed on to the next stage of his descent, but certain in any case that the other could not see the tiny glow that was following him even if he cared to look back.

Ahead of him, Joth saw a quick flicker of light which died away to a soft glow almost imperceptible to his retuned eyes.

At the end of the pathway in the dust was a circular hole in the floor. A cover which had been clamped to it had been removed to one side. Another windlass was positioned beside the hole—bigger and stronger than the one which Burstone had used to lower the suitcase from the catwalk. It was whirring softly—operating automatically. Joth guessed that the strong double chain which unwound with leisurely steadiness supported a cage or basket of some kind, in which both Burstone and the suitcase were riding. They were on their way to the Underworld—to the surface of the ancient Earth.

Joth switched off his torch. The soft pearl-white glow which limned the black rim of the hole surprised him. He had always thought of the Underworld as being pitch dark. He reached up to adjust his eyes, setting them to take the maximum benefit from the light of the Underworld's stars.

He got down on to his hands and knees and crept close to the lip of the hole. He looked into the Underworld, from the viewpoint of one of its own stars.

He could see a long way...hills, forests of weird fleshy plants, intermingled with others of a squatter, more varied nature.

Wilderness, broken and confused, but most definitely not dead. Very much alive, even rich. But he could see no sign of human habitation. Except, perhaps, for the low and even ridge which ran alongside a stretch of water away to his right. That might...just *might*...be a wall.

Far below him, the cage was still descending.

Joth nodded, reassuring himself that all was well. Then he readjusted his eyes, switched on the ultraviolet torch, and looked around for somewhere convenient to hide.

8.

Burstone and Ermold haggled for an hour or more—though the time meant little or nothing to the man of the Underworld. Two warriors from Walgo, Fortex and Theogon, gave some desultory help to Ermold in his arguments, but were really only along for the ride.

The girl, on the other hand, was something different. Burstone had never seen the girl before. She was tied to Ermold—actually, physically tied. The cord was round her neck and his wrist. Occasionally, when she thought Ermold wasn't paying any attention, she would pick at the cord with her fingernails. Ermold usually caught on and swatted her within a minute or so. Once he kicked her.

From Burstone's point of view, the haggling was virtually a waste of time. It always dragged on too long. But he stood to gain nothing by it—the price he received for the goods in the case went to the supplier. So far as he was concerned, the material transaction was just an exchange of garbage. He was in it for quite different reasons. For the experience, in fact.

The girl was interesting. The girl could make this whole trip worthwhile. Her presence did something for the occasion, though none of the men ever mentioned her or referred to her presence. Burstone never touched her, never attempted to talk to her and never asked any questions about her, but he was aware of her, and aware of the cord which attached her to Ermold, which she seemed resolved to break. Ermold was breaking her in. He was a sadist.

The warrior had aged quite noticeably over the last couple

of intervals. It seemed such a short time ago that he had been, by Burstone's standards of judgment, a young man. Now he was past middle age. Time moved faster in the Underworld, if it could be said to move at all. Men aged faster, packed up their lives more economically, wound up their existence more tightly.

Ermold's voice was cracked, he punctuated all his sentences with curses, and his temper seemed inordinately short. Burstone carried a gun, of course, but he knew that Ermold and his men were fast enough to have him in slices before he could kill one of them. So he was frightened. He fed on that fear, as if it was his only pleasure.

Burstone gathered from the excess of bitterness and nastiness which flowed out of Ermold that the chieftain was sick of the whole silly business. But both men knew that Ermold couldn't do without Burstone, and in the end he had to accept Burstone's terms. If there had been any alternative at all...but there wasn't.

So Ermold fingered the sharp edge of his knife—a knife which Burstone had provided for him—and thought dark thoughts, indulging himself in crude fantasies of what he might do to the man from Heaven...but dared not.

In the end, however, the deal was completed, and the two parties went their separate ways. Burstone took his parcel, Ermold made Fortex carry the heavy suitcase.

Hauling himself back up to the Overworld was a long and laborious job. The hoist was properly counterbalanced and the machinery was in perfect order, but Burstone had seen a gradual deterioration in the performance of the machine over a period of time. Whether the decline was due to a failure of the operating mechanism or a failure of his own patience he was not sure. He was not mechanically minded.

Up at the top, in the roof of the Underworld and the deepest cellars of Euchronia, Burstone carefully secured the hoist and clamped the circular cap over the hole. He lit a flicker briefly to make sure of the exact direction of the path back to the ladder. It was a cursory, almost unnecessary gesture motivated by long habit. Normally he let the flame sputter for only a couple of seconds. This time, it lasted longer while he noticed the second set of footprints which led away from his doorway into Hell.

Then, giving no indication of the fact that he knew someone else was there, or that he cared, he walked away into the darkness.

9.

Half an hour later he came back. The hoist was down, the cables were slack. He wound the cage back up again, and found to his utmost satisfaction that it arrived empty. He secured it for a second time, clamped down the cover, and ignited his flicker for a couple of seconds. Then he walked away. This time he went all the way back up to the sunlit spaces of the civilized world, wondering whether his route was still viable.

Whoever had followed him was trapped in the world below. It was some time before he would be making another trip, and the spy would undoubtedly be dead long before then. The only problem was whether anyone else knew about him and, if so, why they were interested.

10.

The Underworld did not, of course, begin all at once. The eclipse of the old surface by the new was a gradual affair, taking several thousands of years. What is more, the platform which was to become the Overworld was started in several sections. Thus the perimetric borderlines between the two worlds were both extensive and slow-moving.

Gradually, the life-system of Earth moved across those borders. Under each section of the covered world some kind of ecosystem survived from the ancient world. The surface was already spoiled and communities of organisms had been in a state of dynamic imbalance for some time before the light of the sun was gradually cut out. The extra pressure imposed by the theft of the sun was great, but not ultimately decisive. When the sections of the platform joined up, so did the two struggling—and not necessarily similar—communities which had grown beneath them. The comingling of the communities induced competition and complementation, and assisted the evolutionary adaptation of the new whole.

Homo sapiens was the species which adapted most easily to the new régime, and by his active interference he encouraged and assisted many other species to do likewise. Not all men belonged to Euchronia. Some preferred their own concept of freedom: freedom from a plan which would demand their total commitment and pay them—individually speaking—absolutely nothing. There were a good many men who regarded the New World as a dream—castles in the air—and who thought it both right and wise to commit themselves to the Old World, and to dedicate themselves to making what they could of it.

Despite a certain amount of mutual dislike and resentment, a good deal of trade went on between the Euchronians and the Groundmen for many centuries while the platform was under construction. Without the food supplies, and to a lesser extent the mineral supplies provided by the men who were committed to the ground, the early years would have been far more difficult for the Planners. But as the platform grew, it grew over the lands which were used by the Groundmen—and it swallowed up the lands of the cooperative just as it swallowed up the lands of the hostile. For many centuries there was a bitter war fought on the expanding frontiers of the Overworld. The Men of the Old World thought they had dealt fairly with Euchronia, and that the theft of their sun was the harshest of evil treatment. The Euchronians believed that the Plan was all-important, that there could be no compromises, and they offered the only compensation they had to offer to all those on the ground—the opportunity to join the Plan. Most of the Groundmen refused, and most of them migrated before the advancing world of darkness, until there was nowhere else left to run, except to the islands which were too tiny to interest the Planners. Many of the islands were already incapable of sustaining human life—there was a poor living to be made from the desolated sea—and many more became so as the hordes descended on their shores. Some island colonies were successful, but for the vast majority of men there were only two choices which mattered: Heaven and Hell. When the platform finally closed its grip on the world, the larger number capitulated, and ascended to Heaven and commitment to the Plan (which was still millennia away from completion). A substantial number, however—perhaps a surprising number— stayed with the Old World, accepting the pale electric stars as a permanent substitute for the garish sun. Their motives were many, and usually mixed. Bitterness and sheer hatred for the Planners were prominent, but not paramount. The dominant reason for the human race refusing to quit the Old World was a commitment to it and an identification with it that was as powerful as the commitment of Euchronia to its Plan.

The Old World was past redemption in terms of the human civilization which had grown up in it. But that did not mean that life was doomed to extinction, nor even that there was any real-istic possibility that life would become extinct. It merely meant that most of the old species had to die, and that hitherto unim-portant species would become vital to the system, and also that new species would have to be discovered. A whole new contract for the interaction of life with environment had to be drawn up and negotiated—negotiated largely (but not entirely, thanks to the presence of man) by trial and error.

The lowest stratum of the biotic hierarchy, the stratum of primary production, underwent the greatest changes. The priority enjoyed by photosynthetic forms was lost. Plant evolu-tion virtually abandoned the angiosperms and reverted to a more primitive state in order to rebuild. The stars were vital in that they allowed the bridge a small extra margin, but in the end they were quite useless as sources of energy (save to a few fugitive species of little importance). Their only real function was to provide for the senses of much higher organisms—man, in particular.

Obviously, it was the fungi and the nonphotosynthetic algae which proved most readily adaptable to the new conditions. They underwent an evolutionary renaissance with great alacrity.

The specialists of the second stratum—the primary consumers—went the way of their diet. The generalists, however, simply reordered their personal priorities. Man had no chance at all of saving the cow, the sheep, or the hen, but he could and did save the pig.

In the higher strata, the percentage devastation decreased serially. Secondary consumers tended to be much less particular than primaries, and had an advantage because of the relative success of some primary species. The more secondaries that were successful, the easier it became for the tertiaries. There was change in the higher regions of life's hierarchy—of course there was change—but there was a relatively low level of extinction. In terms of appearance, change was slow but eventually drastic, but in terms of evolutionary continuity there was nothing like the cataclysmic reorganization suffered in the lower strata. Only the specialist insectivores and some of the carnivores disappeared from the scene that was visible to the naked eye. Microbiotically, things were slightly more complicated, but the principle remained the same.

The omnivores were in no real trouble (in terms of racial survival) at any time. Any species which had survived the rigors of the second dark age was unlikely to be troubled by the roofing of the world. Man's ancient allies the cat and the dog both survived—but independently of man. His ancient rivals, the rat and the cockroach, also survived—indeed, they thrived.

Extinction was responsible for very few of the changes which took place in the tertiary strata. Adaptation, on the other hand, demanded that vast changes in behavioral patterns—and often vast changes in physical form—must take place.

Under the circumstances of such a vast reorganization evolution was permitted—forced, in fact—to work very quickly indeed. The rate of evolution, not just in one or a group of species but throughout the life-system, passed into tachytelic mode.

Evolution by natural selection can be immensely costly. In order to replace erstwhile-useful genes by now-useful genes, vast numbers of individuals in a number of generations have to die. The load on the species becomes tremendous. This demands great fecundity and the acceptance of a very high mortality rate. When unusual requirements are placed on a species the gross numbers of that species inevitably shrink. The more the numbers shrink the faster the turnover of genes proceeds. But there is a threshold beyond which the species cannot replenish itself no matter how fast its rate of evolution. At or near that threshold the evolutionary process is capable of incredible bursts of change. Below it, extinction becomes inevitable and the species dies amid a truly frantic burst of adaptive attempts. If, however, the evolutionary burst at threshold is successful in providing a whole new schema of adaptation *without* taking the absolute numbers of the standing population too low, the evolutionary burst is followed by a rapid increase in numbers, during which selection still continues to foster a rate of evolution faster than the "normal" horotelic mode characteristic of a stable species in a stable environment. Relatively rare species with a high degree of genetic homogeneity existing in ultra-stable environments may slip into the third mode of evolutionary pace—the bradytelic—whereby change slows down drastically and the species retains little capacity for change.

During the thousands of years that the Euchronians were taking their Plan to ultimate completion the tachytelic evolution which embraced the entire Underworld life-system completely changed the face of the lower Earth. A few thousand years is a very brief interval in evolutionary terms but the circumstances were highly unusual, and the process was—to some extent—stimulated and guided by the efforts of mankind. Man himself was by no means immune from the changes he helped to bring about, and the human race—or races, to be strictly accurate—which survived in the Underworld were very different in many ways from the race which survived up above. Even that race—Euchronian man—underwent some evolution during the millennia of the Plan, for the circumstances of that race also necessitated a rate of change somewhat higher than horotelic.

By the time the Euchronian Millennium began, the Underworld had slowed in its evolutionary progress. But the stable horotelic rate which was becoming characteristic of that world was by no means the same as the horotelic rate in the Overworld. In the Underworld there was still a régime of rigorous competition demanding evolutionary divergence. In addition to that there was an extra, and by no means insignificant, load imposed by the high frequency of mutation. The radiation output of the Overworld was directed downwards. Radioactive wastes were disposed of down below, and though they were carefully packaged the rate of leakage was high.

Man—omnivorous, intelligent and at the very highest level of the biotic hierarchy—changed least of the species at that level, and even the human race suffered a tripartite sub-speciation. The species which changed most were the semi-intelligent species which had cohabited with man the concrete jungles of the age of psychosis. Such species had been under considerable adaptive pressure for some centuries before the advent of Euchronia's Plan. Under the new régime that pressure burst the conceptual barriers which hindered mind development, and three species quickly evolved intelligence of an unusual order.

While the Euchronians began their new life after the Plan had been brought to a successful conclusion, the people of the Underworld were still faced with a fearsome struggle for existence. While the one world settled down to embrace total stability, the other remained in a state of virtual chaos.

11.

The Marriage of Heaven and Hell by Carl Magner became available at all household lineprinters and the usual public outlets within a matter of minutes after the job of coding it into the cybernet was complete. The information that the book was so available took a little longer to circulate, and even then there was no mad rush to have a look at it.

Many people misinterpreted the use of a well-known title by William Blake. It was by no means uncommon in Euchronia's Millennium for people to write long commentaries on, and even new versions of, prehistoric literature. After all, the essence and the meaning of ancient works had changed completely in the light of brand new Euchronian perspectives, and there was an eleven-thousand-year gap in the more abstract realms of cultural studies to be intellectually bridged. The assumption that Magner's work was intimately connected with Blake's was not unnatural. It is entirely possible that some of the men and women who did read the book soon after publication actually misread the whole text on the basis of that presumed connection. It is not inconceivable that given a decent interval and a certain amount of wayward luck Magner might have become something of a literary phenomenon, hailed as a genius in some quarters and viciously slandered in others.

But the *avant-garde* missed their chance (or Magner missed his). It was not too long before it was realized that the work stood by itself, that what it proposed was real, and that Magner actually meant what he said. This revelation caused something of a stir, but it was a stir of an entirely different kind.

The book gave a detailed account of life in the Underworld as it was lived by the human race. The account was possessed of a strange kind of hysteria, and the images presented lacked overall coherency though they had undoubted force and individual clarity. Many readers came to the conclusion that Magner was, if nothing else, a consummate artist. The bizarre and the terrifying were not common in the literature of the Euchronian Millennium.

The book also presented a strongly worded argument to the effect that Euchronia was guilty of extreme inhumanity In that it chose not to share its wealth with the men on the ground. Magner claimed that Euchronian civilization should not have shut the door on the Underworld when the platform became a single unit. He claimed that the opportunity to join the Movement should have been made available throughout the history of the Plan.

He further claimed that the citizens of the Euchronian Millennium had a moral obligation to throw open the doors to the Underworld, to resume commerce with the men on the ground, to supply their needs, and to allow them—if they wished—to leave the Underworld and take their place in the sun. "We have no right whatsoever," wrote Magner, "to deny the people of the world below the Face of Heaven."

12.

It was some two weeks after publication that the Magner affair began to get off the ground. The man who initiated the *cause célèbre* was Alwyn Ballow, a software processer for the holovisual network. He took it to Yvon Emerich, who was *the* major influence in the live media.

Emerich was a busy man. He was a man with a burning need to *keep* himself busy, to burn himself out. He had a great deal of energy to expend and he expended it all outwards, sending it worldwide throughout the network, throwing his sound and fury into every household which cared to switch him on. The sheer power of his extrovert determination was enough to command him a vast audience. He had innumerably more enemies than friends, but his enemies loved him more than his closest allies. He had nothing to offer friends but everything to offer enemies—people luxuriated in the charisma of his attacks, and he attacked everybody, tearing down all points of view with equal verve. No one really suffered from an attack by Emerich simply because in the *laissez-faire* world of the Millennium no one had the level of commitment necessary to suffer destruction at his hands. Argument was a gladitorial game, in which the loser changed his ground and everybody enjoyed the show.

Ballow was scared stiff of Emerich, but he was willing enough to absorb his fear if he could start something in motion. He confronted Emerich and came straight to the point.

"The Marriage of Heaven and Hell," he said.

"What about it?" demanded Emerich.

"Have you read it?"

"You know damn well I never read anything. I know what it's about. What the hell would I want with it?"

"It's good."

"Call Sauldron. He's an arts man."

"Not that sort of good," Ballow persisted. "Good for a run. It's got one hell of a bite—the first real bite we've seen for a long time. Could be the biggest ever."

"The man's a lunatic," said Emerich shortly—though the fact that he was prepared to argue meant that he was prepared to listen and take note—"and you can't make a big thing out of a lunatic. In the end, a lunatic will make you look a fool. Every time. No percentage."

"No," said Ballow. "This proposal might be insane but it has mileage. It's going to attract some pretty hot discussion at *all* levels. If we can get in now we can carve up that discussion and feed it. It'll go right to the top, and I mean the top. The Eupsychians will take it up purely as agitation, but it's not really a Eupsychian thing. It goes deeper. When this gets to the Hegemony they're going to find that it's hot. It can't be ignored and it can't be laughed off. Heres and his cohort have been retreating toward the wall for forty years or more now and it won't take much more to break their back. This could be it, if it's blown up enough. Somebody somewhere is going to try, and try hard. And we ought to be in there to feed on it. This is our meat, Yvon, provided it's handled right."

Emerich stared at the other man for a few seconds, and then made up his mind. "Okay," he said, and cut the image. The voiceprinter screen faded to dull gray. Emerich remained staring at it for a few seconds more. He was hooked. He would have to chase it if only to find out what the hell Ballow was talking about.

He requisitioned a couple of copies from his desk unit, and scanned the first few pages as they fluttered out of the lineprinter. He grimaced dramatically, and dropped the printout with distaste. He reached for the voiceprinter again. He would have to find someone to read it for him.

13.

Having predicted that something was going to start as a result of Magner's book, Ballow was fully committed to doing everything in his power to start it, and thus justify his prediction. He began calling his valued acquaintances in all fields of work as soon as Emerich cut him off. Nobody he called had read the book, and few of them would bother to catch up on it as a result of his recommendation. But most of them would be prepared to talk about it if it was going to become a big talking point.

Within a matter of hours Ballow had precipitated something of a rush on *The Marriage*. Lineprinters in the most unlikely corners of the world were busy clicking out copies at a furious pace. Not many of the copies would be read from beginning to end, but everybody who intended to involve themselves in the debate wanted to have some familiarity with the shape of the work and the style of presentation.

There was something of a snowball effect when the cybernet made it known that there was expanding interest in the book. The controversy grew by leaps and bounds as individuals selected standpoints and prepared for argument. The promotion of the book to a position of some importance was almost entirely a matter of fashion. It was all something of a game. In the wake of the Euchronian Plan there was not much else it could be. *Everything* was a game, now the Plan was done with. When a single-minded people lose the objective of eleven thousand years of completely focused purpose, it takes time to rediscover anything like a *range* of purpose and endeavor. The whole of life and action is reduced to triviality, and the whole structure of social action has to be rebuilt from the ground up.

The citizens of Euchronia's Millennium had to *evolve* into their new circumstances, and in the strategic absence of virtually all basic social pressures, that evolution was not something which could take place overnight. There had to be some form of struggle to find new things to *need*—not simply to want—and the context of that struggle made it a very difficult one. Euchronia became a world of children and eccentrics the moment the Plan was laid to rest. The Hegemony of the Movement were not surprised—they accepted that a long period of adjustment would be necessary. Indeed, they welcomed the fact, because it gave them a chance to plan the kind of adjustment which would evolve, and it gave them time to fulfill their aim of shaping a stable society. Their work on the physical environment was over, but their work on the human factor was only just begun. By the time that Magner's book was published they had made very little progress indeed (some would have argued that they made none, or less than none) but they were prepared to be generous with time. They still had faith—perfect faith. Again, that was the legacy of eleven thousand years' commitment.

Thus, though Ballow was not an important man, he found it fairly easy to make an issue out of Magner's ideas. If he had not, someone else would have. They were, when all was said and done, rather revolutionary ideas. The fact that virtually no one took Magner seriously in the beginning did not handicap the progress of his work towards popularity (notoriety, at least). And it was inevitable in a world which so desperately needed *some* kind of ideological commitment that he should gradually begin to win supporters.

The snowball grew, and Magner moved ponderously into the political arena.

14.

Rafael Heres was by no means pleased when Enzo Ulicon took it into his head to demand an instant discussion of Carl Magner's *The Marriage of Heaven and Hell.*

"I'm in the middle of a game of Hoh," he said, his tone making it quite clear that he resented the interruption.

"Postpone it," said Ulicon.

"I'll lose all semblance of control over the situation," said Heres. "What about the others? They aren't going to take kindly to the interruption."

"Rafael," said Ulicon, "you're the Hegemon. You can't fit the running of the world into the interstices of your social life. There's a storm brewing."

"Don't be ridiculous," said Heres. "This business of opening the Underworld is a farce. It's all under control. It's just a nonsensical argument thrown up to confuse the *real* problems we have to face."

"You aren't going to solve *any* problems playing Hoh," Ulicon pointed out. "I have to talk to you. This is urgent. It's not just talk any more. This thing is touching one of the most fundamental of our problems. *The* most fundamental."

"What do you mean?"

"Interrupt your game and I'll tell you."

Heres, reluctantly, phased himself out of the game, leaving the other players to carry on without him or to let the game go cold while they awaited his return, as they pleased. When he was alone—switched out of the other call circuits, that is— he gave his full attention to Ulicon. He was still wearing his displeasure prominently.

"What is it?" he snapped.

"I've been trying to find out where Magner gets his information," said Ulicon. "He's pretty close-mouthed about it. There are no sources offered in the book or in any of the associated material."

"Magner's son went down there."

"He didn't come back, so far as I can tell. Nor did any of the others. I've conducted a fairly thorough search. If they were using the net they'd be easy to find, but they're not. They could be in Sanctuary, but every source I have says that they aren't. There are four of them—and it's not easy for four men to stay unfound up here. Everything suggests that they went into the Underworld and are still there. In addition, Magner's other son—the younger one—has also slipped out of sight. You may remember the fuss there was about him when he was a child. Anyhow, he's gone too. But Magner hasn't contacted either of them since we first mounted our watch."

"Are you saying that he made it all up?"

"It's a possibility," said Ulicon, "but no, I'm not saying that. I heard a rumor which was much more significant, and I've checked with Magner's doctor. He wouldn't tell me anything directly, but with police help I got some records out of the net. Magner has been consulting his doctor regularly for twenty years. He complains of bad dreams. Nightmares."

"That's not possible," said Heres.

"It's possible, bearing in mind what Magner went through with regard to his younger son. But rumor says that Magner's picture of the Underworld comes straight out of his dreams, and if that's so it's a fact we can't ignore. It's a fact with some rather weighty implications. We need to find out for certain, but what's more important is to decide what we have to do if it *is* true."

"Nothing," said Heres. "It's absurd. It can only be a freak even if it's true. We're hardly likely to have an epidemic of nightmares."

"I'm glad you're sure," said Ulicon. "But it still needs checking."

"You want a meeting of the close council?"

"Naturally."

"Couldn't we keep it between ourselves?"

"Rafael, it's bad enough the close council keeping secrets from the Hegemony, without keeping secrets from one another.

All right, I know this will give ammunition to Eliot, but believe me, if the implications of this are as bad as they might be, then Eliot has a strong case. We have to work this out. All of us."

"When?" said Heres.

"Tomorrow. A forgathering. This can't go through the net. We need to talk off the record. But in the meantime I'm going to do some prying and I advise you to do the same. Emerich's on to Magner and there's going to be a splash soon. If this business of dreams crops up and Magner *isn't* the only one, then we have a very big headache indeed. You see?"

Heres saw perfectly clearly. His mind was already working on the point. The implications of Ulicon's argument were deadly, not only to his own personal position, but to the standpoint of the Euchronian Movement.

15.

The basis of Euchronianism is the philosophy that better things lie ahead. The Euchronian Movement was founded on the principle of directing change, not on a small scale, but on the largest scale possible. The Euchronian Movement preached the doctrine that to design a model society and predict that it would one day come about was simply not enough. The Movement demanded commitment—commitment to an ideal state which lay so far in the future that no man would live to see it, nor his children, nor his children's children—only descendants so remote that they might number half the human race. The Movement demanded ultimate sacrifice in the name of a goal which could only be a racial goal.

William Blake's "prophetic books" offered the first Euchronian philosophy.

Karl Marx's social science offered the first Euchronian doctrine.

Fundamental to Euchronianism is the intellectual transcendence of pure selfishness. Euchronianism is not necessarily religious, nor is it necessarily socialist. It is, however, necessarily altruistic.

16.

Cudal Canal, for the whole of its length, marked the boundary of the land of the Men Without Souls and the land of the Children of the Voice which had come to be called Shairn. It was a natural boundary, and one which nobody was particularly keen to dispute, but over the centuries walls of earth and stone had been erected on either side to emphasize it and to allow some sort of defense of it if the need arose. The canal itself was a vile place—its water was undrinkable and even the crabs would not use it—and the land on either side of it was diseased and swarming with flying insects. It was land that was crossed only by wanderers and invaders. But once now and again it became necessary for a meeting to take place in the neutral territory—a meeting between the Men Without Souls and the Children of the Voice. The former usually came out from Walgo, the latter from Stalhelm.

The Men Without Souls often hit hard times, and when times became too hard they had no alternative but to turn toward Shairn for food. The Children of the Voice managed crops on a large scale and rarely went short of food, even when the migrations threatened to starve them of meat. In peaceful times the men from Walgo would trade regularly with Stalhelm, offering fish and tools for grain and bricks. But times were rarely peaceful, and Ermold of Walgo was by no means a peaceful man. Trade had ceased during the time of his reign, and the meetings by Cudal Canal were rare—forced by necessity upon Ermold's people.

Because Ermold's people were the ones with the dire need the meetings at the canal usually resulted in the better side of the bargain going to Stalhelm. This only made Ermold hate such occasions all the more. When he desperately needed Shairn's grain he had to pay not in fish or other standard trade goods, but in Heaven-metal and Heaven-sent books. Because Shairn had no independent source of such things, and because the Children of the Voice were lovers of books and efficient tools, such things were always in high demand. But the Children of the Voice were prepared to go without if need be, and could afford to. The pressure was always on Ermold, and he resented that. Often he would try to raid Stalhelm and steal supplies rather than buy them, but such fighting was always costly and bitter, and the invaders rarely managed to carry off anything like what they needed. It had become clear to Ermold that it was easier and better to trade with the Children of the Voice first and *then* raid—to steal what he could and to make him feel better anyway. Stalhelm knew of this thinking, and they made him pay all the more in consequence. It was accepted in Stalhelm that while Ermold ruled there would inevitably be the worst of bad blood between the peoples on either side of Cudal Canal.

Ermold and his men had to cross the filthy water to attend the meeting, and they spent some time making sure that they could do so without getting their feet wet—and that they could get back in a hurry if need be.

The chieftain of Walgo positioned three or four of his best men behind Shairn's wall, supported by a rough and ready pontoon, and then he went forward into Shairn, accompanied only by Fortex and—of course—the girl named Huldi, who was still secured to him by the cord.

He watched the Children of the Voice coming slowly downhill towards him.

"Filthy scavengers," he muttered. "Filthy, disgusting little beasts." Ermold was not a very big man by the standards of his people, though he was broad and immensely powerful. His height was closer to the average of the Children of the Voice, and the worst insult that could be hurled at him was well-known among his people. He had killed people for calling him "Shairan" and he would probably have gone berserk if he had heard anyone use the word "Rat." The insults of his elders during his childhood probably had much to do with his deep-seated hatred of his neighbors.

"That gray meat they bring will be full of cockroaches," he said to Fortex. "It's what they wouldn't eat themselves. And they think it's good enough for *men*. I'll have a few skulls before this affair is quit. If I could only get near Old Man Yami...."

"He's not with them," said Fortex, in a low voice. "It's his son. Camlak. I wonder whether he's killed the old one."

"*That* one!" snarled Ermold. "A coward if ever I saw one. If *he's* Old Man in Stalhelm we won't need to go hungry for a while. I could eat him alive."

"He'll not be Old Man," said Fortex glumly. "He'll be here under orders. When Yami's finished they'll get a new leader. A strong one."

"They don't have that much sense," said Ermold. He was optimistic only by virtue of the strength of his hatred.

The girl was picking at the cord with her teeth. His attention had wavered. He kicked her in the belly and checked the strength of the cord.

Fortex wondered—privately—what the Shaira were going to think of Ermold having to keep his woman on a string, but he would never have dared to make such a thought known.

There were six men from Stalhelm, and each of them carried a basket filled with dried asci from the gray-green saporshafts which they tended in some of their fields. In Ermold's lands, they grew wild, but the supply was almost gone. Six baskets was little enough to distribute among the people of Walgo, but there would be more in time and time after if things went well today. A meeting of this kind could drag on and on before a serious squabble developed. Terms of exchange were always agreed at the first encounter, but they rarely held good forever, or even for long enough for Ermold to lay in anything of a store. Something always went sour.

Ermold half-turned. "Bring the box," he commanded.

The suitcase was passed over the wall, and Fortex stepped back to collect it. It no longer contained all that it had when

Burstone brought it into the world—some of the knives and implements would never find their way into Stalhelm, the books and the rest of the steel would have to be eked out and supplemented with such junk as Ermold thought he could pass off.

Huldi began biting at the cord once again.

Camlak came forward from his party and stood some six or ten feet away from Ermold. The warriors from Walgo stood up, stretching themselves to the full extent of their height to emphasize their superiority. Huldi stood up too. She was bigger than Ermold. He jerked the cord and made her fall back on to her haunches.

"Where's Yami?" demanded Ermold.

"Sick," said Camlak.

"Sick of a steel blade," suggested Ermold.

"Just sick," insisted Camlak, refusing to be intimidated by size or anything else. Porcel and the other warriors were watching him closely. This might well turn out to be something of a test.

Ermold let out a sound that was midway between a laugh and a belch. He threw the suitcase at Camlak's feet. "That's worth twenty baskets," he said. "You can take away the books one at a time and bring more gray meat. Later, we'll bring you more. Just keep the meat coming."

Camlak opened the case and inspected the contents.

"Six," he said. "You want more than we brought, you bring more. I take it all now."

Ermold went into the old routine. It was new to Camlak but the younger man obviously knew what to expect. He had inherited little enough from his father, but he did have patience. And from his own point of view as well as the point of view of his people, he could not afford to take less than he might get. Ermold tried hard, but got nowhere. The trouble was that Ermold *expected* Camlak to take less than his father would have, and when the young man proved just as obstinate Ermold became very angry.

The haggling grew intense, and then fierce. A genuine gap was open between each man's final price—or what each man thought his final price ought rightly to be. Camlak had every intention of sticking by his—he was prepared to take the asci home if he had to—and Ermold's temper boiled as this became more and more obvious.

Meanwhile, Huldi had gone to work with a sharp stone, and had succeeded in scratching apart most of the threads in the cord which bound her. While she sawed she wondered exactly what she was going to do when the string finally parted. She knew that she could only take rebellion against Ermold's anger and lust so far, and that in the present circumstances the simple fact of getting free was liable to be more than far enough. She had to run fast, and she had to have somewhere to run. She dared not go back toward Walgo while Ermold lived, and so it seemed that she had to cross Shairn—or persuade the Shaira to shelter her. That was not unknown—there were always odd Soulless Men and Hellkin hanging around the towns of Shairn, and in Central Shairn they would hardly be likely to hold it against her that she came from troublesome Walgo. Ermold's trouble was limited in scope.

While she sawed she looked speculatively at Camlak and his followers, and flicked occasional anxious glances back at Fortex. She could sense a fight building up and she knew which side she was on. She only hoped *they* would realize it fast enough.

The rope parted just as Ermold was in the process of yielding to his temper. It was an unfortunate coincidence that at the very moment of parting he was jerking his right arm in a gesture of anger and petulance. The loose end of the rope flipped up into the air and distracted Ermold at the crucial second. His knife was already half-drawn, and the one time that momentary surprise is invariably fatal is when it catches a man with his weapon half-drawn.

Camlak got to him first. The small man had a knife up his sleeve, and he didn't even have to stand up. The blade was in Ermold's abdomen just below the navel before he had time to think. It was a vicious wound, but the knife was far too small for it to be mortal. Ermold went down in a heap and lay still, waiting for the arrows to fly over his head. Camlak was already hauling out a deadlier weapon and the other warriors were coming forward.

Ermold howled.

Fortex howled too and launched himself on Camlak, brandishing a great stone axe. Ermold's spare warriors popped up over the wall, bowstrings stretched. Fortex landed beside Huldi, but his attention was completely fixed on Camlak. That was a mistake. Huldi sprang up and brought her left arm round in a long arc. The sharp stone carved a gaping hole in the side of Fortex's neck, and his carotid spouted blood.

One of Walgo's bowmen caught a spear in his right eye and was hurled backwards into the water. It was a blow directed by sheer fortune. The other Men Without Souls unleashed their arrows harmlessly, counted up the odds, and fled, bounding back across their pontoon and making for Walgo with all possible speed.

Camlak was astonished. He stared at Huldi, holding his long dagger as if he had half a mind to run her through. His mind was made up by Ermold, who grabbed him by the ankles and upended him before leaping to his feet, hurling his own knife at the nearest of Camlak's men, and taking flight. No doubt he would have loved to kill Huldi before he went, but there was no time. Nor was there any chance of getting back to his own side of the canal. He set off along the Shairn bank in the shadow of the wall. A couple of arrows followed him, missed, and then he disappeared with a crash into a tall clump of clawreeds.

Porcel and the other warriors never paused to wonder if they should await orders from their Old Man's son. They were after Ermold like a pack of hounds. They knew he was wounded and the thought of his being allowed to get away and recover from his wound was patently intolerable.

Camlak was the only one who stayed. He got to his feet and stared warily at Huldi, who was still there, waiting.

"You're not going after him?" she said.

Camlak shook his head. "I've got what I came for."

He picked up the suitcase, and carefully fastened the locks. He sheathed his dagger, and set out for Stalhelm—walking slowly. Huldi followed him. As they walked past the group of baskets filled with gray meat, Camlak kicked them over.

A swarm of flies was not long gathering over the meat, and over the bodies.

17.

Julea sat at the dressing table, inspecting herself critically in the mirror.

She looked too young to have sent her brother to his death. One of her brothers. The other had gone of his own accord.

Downstairs, she could hear the argument beginning. She bit her lower lip, and continued adjusting her hair. The argument had begun so many times, by now, and had never yet reached any semblance of an ending. Tonight's version, at least, was to be private, and one had to be thankful for that.

Somehow, she could no longer see her father as the hero of the affair. She believed in him, after a fashion, but she could no longer commit herself in any way at all to the storm which was building up around him. There had been a storm before, shortly after she was born. She had grown up in the shadow of that storm, alongside Joth. Joth was dead now. She had sent him to follow Ryan, and he had. It must have been madness on her part. She must have known, underneath, that he would meet the same fate, whatever it was.

She looked at herself in the mirror, and accused herself of murder.

The charge wasn't fair, but the guilt still massed in her mind. She had lost so much, in a world where loss was so rare, and so immaterial. No one else could possibly understand how she felt.

While Carl Magner angled for one more convert, his daughter played out her private melodrama.

They were saying that her father was mad, and she had

begun to listen to them, if not to believe them. She felt some guilt about that as well.

When she had finished attending to her hair she sat still for a few moments more, still fascinated by her own tragic image in the mirror. It was trying hard to be an alien face, to cast itself in the role of accuser or accused so that her feelings could be polarized at least in her illusions. She felt almost as though her identity were shattering slowly. All the things which had conspired to maintain it were dying or dead.

Carl Magner was one of the dying. His sons were the dead.

She had bad dreams herself now. But nothing like her father's. Just disturbed dreams, in which images of Ryan and Joth and the world competed for her guilt and erased her part in the fabric of being.

She simply could not understand what was happening. Worse, she had no idea *why*.

She blanked the mirror and went downstairs.

18.

Abram Ravelvent was one of the cognoscenti. He was a scientist—a man of knowledge.

Knowledge is not wisdom, and nowhere was that more obvious than in the character of Abram Ravelvent.

He looked old—his hair was gray, his complexion dark. His skin had the visual texture of horn. Yet he had fifty more years in him yet, if he was careful and moderately fortunate.

He was barely turned ninety. The look of antiquity was cultivated—it had been carefully brought out over the years, matured, remodeled, set hard and firm. The look of the all-knowing. The look, also, of the verbal *chevalier*, the argumentative artist.

Ravelvent had no influence save for his personality, but nevertheless he would be one of the most valuable additions to the Magner bandwagon if he could be persuaded to climb aboard.

He was at least willing to be persuaded, but he had come armed with arguments which he believed to be infallible. He intended to refute Magner's case entirely, just to show that he could do it. Then, if the prospect seemed attractive, he might become Magner's ally in the campaign to have the Underworld opened.

His infallible argument, fairly simply stated, was that *The Marriage of Heaven and Hell* could not possibly be true.

19.

"Why not?" said Magner, brusquely. "Explain to me. Why not?"

"It's a naïve picture," said Ravelvent. "It simply does not take into account the rigorousness and the essential alien-ness of any life-system which could survive in the conditions as they must be down there. Without light, the primary energy-source is likely to be heat. What you are proposing, therefore, in your portrait of life as lived by the people of the Underworld, is the evolution of an entirely thermosynthetic plant-kingdom to the level of complexity and efficiency required to sustain higher life-forms in a mere matter of eleven thousand years. It's simply not possible."

"There's an alternative energy source," said Magner.

"These 'stars' that you mention? Really, one can hardly put much credence...."

"Waste," said Magner. "The waste of the Overworld. Our civilization exports millions of tons of raw waste into the Underworld every year. Organic waste of all kinds—waste which is replete with reclaimable energy."

"*We* reclaim a lot of it," Ravelvent pointed out.

"Not so," said Magner. "We reclaim metals, phosphates, nitrates and a few other minor things which are convenient and cheap to reclaim. But with atomic power, solar power, and tidal power in relative abundance we don't need to exploit the waste as an energy source—and that's the way in which the Underworld will exploit it. We take back a very tiny fraction indeed of what we export, as a glance at the figures available through the cybernet will assure you."

"But even if that *is* so," Ravelvent protested, "the principle remains the same. You're proposing an evolutionary proliferation which just isn't possible. You're hypothesizing the death of virtually everything of the old régime, and the growth of an entire replacement system. All right, even if that could happen, even if it has happened, one simply cannot imagine the kind of continuity you imagine to have taken place in human society.

"Look closely at the kind of life which you suppose these people to be living. You imagine them to be loosely grouped into tribes, inhabiting small towns, buildings made of...what? Earth? Mud? Brick? Anyhow, they seem to have agriculture on some scale. They live peacefully for the most part, though they are a strong people. They hunt, but for the most part they use their weapons defensively against large carnivores whose description defies classification. They have other enemies, too, which you also seem to find some difficulty classifying. Humanoid creatures, larger than men, warlike, sometimes masked, sometimes naked, sometimes clothed, sometimes *furred*. What are all these strange beings supposed to be? There is no explanation in your book. But never mind that. What is the sum total of what we have here? An image of man as a kind of noble savage, heroically struggling to maintain a primitive social organization and even primitive social ideals of peace and prosperity against the terrible threats of a hostile environment.

"But this hostile environment does little more than threaten. Most of its threats seem to be ghostly creatures with no sense to them at all. Giants and ape-men. What are they supposed to be? Mutants...?" He paused for a moment, but Magner did not seem anxious to enlighten him at this particular juncture. "Your account makes a strong psychological appeal. It may even make some kind of psychological sense. But scientifically, it is nonsense to suppose that life in the Underworld could be anything like this. If there *are* men alive down there, then they *do* live in an implacably hostile environment. The sheer dereliction of the environment must make searching for food a full-time operation. The notion of agriculture, townships, tribal organization...all these are quite out of the question. Man was and is a product of environment. The men of the Underworld were functionally designed to live in an environment which has very little, if anything, in common with the present environment of the Underworld. The idea of their maintaining the same kind of existence is patently ludicrous.

"If there are men in the Underworld today—and I feel obliged to say *if*—then we cannot rationally imagine that they have anything in common with the men of prehistoric ages, let alone with ourselves. They would not merely be primitives and savages, they would—quite literally—be animals. They would be forced to spend their time providing the bare necessities of survival—food and fecundity. They would be no more human than cattle or, if you would like a more appropriate example, wolves. If they work in groups, the groups are packs and not tribes."

"You paint a very harsh picture," said Magner.

"It is a realistic picture," insisted Ravelvent.

"You seem to have virtually no faith in humanity as a species or the human being as an intelligent, adaptable creature," said Magner.

"Faith! What has *faith* to do with it? We cannot decide what the Underworld is like on the basis of faith. We cannot determine the nature and the abilities of man by wishful thinking. There are *facts* to be taken into consideration. Hard facts which we know to be true. Even as a speculative exercise, we must make full and complete use of the facts in sketching a picture of what life might be like in the world below. Complete fidelity to known science is an absolute necessity in any *proper* use of the imagination. I *know* that the account you give of the Underworld in your book is the product of your imagination purely and simply because you have used that imagination badly. It is an imagination undisciplined by fact. If we *are* to open the Underworld—and I do not believe that proposition to be unreasonable—then we must have a realistic idea of what we are likely to find.

"You seem to think that all that is necessary is for us to throw wide our gates, and the men of the Underworld will queue up to desert their world. Perhaps that is so. It can hardly be doubted that they would find our world a more attractive proposition than theirs, provided that they could stand the sunlight. But you seem to assume that the story ends—happily—there and then. That is patently ridiculous. If these creatures—and I say creatures quite deliberately—come into our world they will not do so as citizens of Euchronian society. They will do so as predators and scavengers—as beasts. In prehistoric days they gave accounts of feral children—men reared as beasts—and they said that such children could not be reeducated to human ways. They could not even be made to walk like men. You are proposing that five hundred generations of feral children can be accepted into the human race just like *that*!

"If we open the Underworld, then we must do so both fore-warned and forearmed. We cannot do so in order to deal in any way whatsoever with the people of the Underworld. Our chief priority must be to explore, to discover, and to evaluate. We are far more likely to find that the rigors of the Underworld are breeding creatures which are a potentially deadly threat to us than men which we can communicate with. We must know about the Underworld, and we cannot afford to turn our backs to it forever. But we must recognize that these anthropocentric ideas of yours are nothing but a tissue of dreams."

Ravelvent stopped, unaware of the effects which his last remark might have had on Carl Magner.

Magner made no immediate reply. In the final analysis, he had nothing with which to argue save conviction, and that was one thing which the people of Euchronia's Millennium could not accept. They did not even know what it was.

"We must send people into the Underworld," said Magner. "A proper expedition *must* be mounted, as soon as possible. This is the first priority. When it returns, then we will all know that what I have said is *true*. Every last detail. I know that there are men in the Underworld who live as I have *seen* them living. We have no right to withhold from them the Face of Heaven."

"I think," said Ravelvent, "that when the truth *is* revealed, it will be closer to the picture that I have drawn."

20.

The basis of Eupsychianism is the philosophy that a better life is to be sought inwardly rather than outwardly.

Eupsychianism is, implicitly, the alternative to and the enemy of Euchronianism. Whereas Euchronian ideals are directed toward collective man, favoring the group rather than the individual, Eupsychian ideals are intrinsically self-centered and self-limited. Euchronianism is an extrovert philosophy, Eupsychianism is introverted.

The essential difference between the two opposing philosophies is not a matter of the extent of freedom, but of the very meaning of freedom.

A Euchronian would claim that a man is the product of his environment, and that the enrichment of a man is attainable purely and simply by the enrichment of his environment. A Euchronian would argue that the perfect freedom is the. freedom to manipulate and shape the environment, the freedom *of* the environment.

A Eupsychian would say that the whole essence of man is the power to transcend his environment, and that capitulation to the forces of the environment is equivalent to the destruction of humanity itself, or at least the subjugation of that humanity to purely mechanical external demands. A Eupsychian would argue that the only true freedom is freedom *from* the environment.

Paradoxically, a Euchronian Utopia would probably be very little different in appearance from a Eupsychian. The difference would lie in its direction of development. The society of the Euchronian Millennium is by no means anathema to the Eupsychians, who form the principal (minority) opposition to the political arm of the Movement proper. The difference between the factions is to do with attitudes to people and the functional design of social institutions rather than with the mechanical components of the civilization. Both factions admit to the machines as the ideal means of providing for the basic needs of survival. But the Euchronians are dedicated to stability—to the management of collective mankind, while the Eupsychians reject any such notion with disdain. They reject all forms of political and social management.

It would be naïve to imagine that the split between the factions as it is reflected in Euchronian society is quite that clear or quite that orderly. Citizens come in all shades of opinion. Not everyone would call himself a Euchronian or a Eupsychian, and two men who accepted the same label might have very different views—not only at a trivial level, but in terms of basic priorities.

However, in the context of the Euchronian Millennium, the polarization of political attitudes may be said to fall along the defined spectrum.

The Euchronians, for the most part, regard the Eupsychians as traitors. There is some justice in this—the Euchronian Movement planned and built the civilization in which they live, and built it by means of absolute dedication on the part of the Plan's participants. In the eyes of the Euchronians, Euchronianism has proved itself absolutely.

The Eupsychians, on the other hand, see the Euchronians as having become redundant on the day the Millennium was declared. There is some justice in this too—the society of the Millennium is ultracomfortable, but it must be admitted that there is a surprising amount of unrest and unhappiness. Despite the fact that no citizen of the Millennium lives in a state of deprivation there is a significant crime rate, and crimes of violence are not uncommon—though the violence involved is usually at a trivial level. Violence against the machines which provide for the populace is also surprisingly common—and this is occasionally not so trivial. The Eupsychians claim that now the priority is no longer survival but freedom, then true freedom must be encouraged, not the Euchronian version. On the other hand, the Euchronians would counter this argument....

The debate, of course, continues.

21.

Joth was panic-stricken.

He was moving through perpetual night, timelessly, going nowhere, with no motive for going.

He had no sense of direction, no sense of distance, no sense of speed. It might almost be said that he had no sense of being. He was not afraid.

Joth had no instinctive reactions. Instinctive reactions had been withheld from him, deliberately and strategically. Instinct would have allowed him to be afraid. It would have given him a context for fear, and the physiological component of the emotion would have mobilized his resources for a fear-reaction. He would have run, but behind his running there would have been an urgent, fear-stimulated consciousness.

Without instinct, Joth was in the grip of panic. There are reactions which go deeper than conditioning, deeper than instinct, deeper even than reflex. Conditioning and instinct are both properties of mind—of mental organization, however primitive. A dog has instinct, a bird has instinct, a fish has instinct. Below mind, there are still mind-like reactions, An amoeba has tropisms, a mollusc has tropisms, even a plant has tropisms. These things too have some component of function in them, of reason. In that sense, Joth's panic had some semblance of reason. When mind is inadequate—totally inadequate—to deal with situation-stimulus, then mind must step aside and allow something deeper to assume control of body. Joth's mind had recoiled when he found himself trapped in the Underworld—recoiled all the way. It had simply denied all responsibility, refused to have any part in determination of events. Joth's actions had passed into the control of something different—something more basic than the essential *him*, his identity.

Joth ran. Hard. He was outside time and outside sensory perception. His ego was in a well of utter, ultimate loneliness. Perhaps beyond space also, isolated from the universe itself. Nowhere. In the oceanic, transcendental regions where the soul lives (if men have souls).

His heart pumped at a furious rate, his muscles sucked up energy at the very limits of their capacity. His limbs levered his body through space without any regard whatsoever for the strain on the ligaments and membranes.

He felt no pain. Yet.

His eyes reflected the gleam of the stars, but did not see. Even so, his headlong flight failed to bring him into collision with any of the pillars which supported the sky, or with any of the impenetrable clumps of vegetation which dotted the ground between them.

Eventually, however, there had to come a time when the body could no longer put up with the demands which were being made upon it. It simply could not meet them. When that happened, Joth collapsed, and he lay still.

Again, the interval was timeless.

When he came to, his mind was once again in his brain. This time, he opened his eyes and he could see the stars in the sky, pale and still. He knew where he was.

He could not move. His whole body was being eaten by pain. He lay face upward in inch-deep mud and slime, and he could feel the wetness all over his back and his legs and the back of his head. There were cockroaches moving over his body, but he could do nothing. He was helpless.

It was as though he was newly born for a second time. He

could remember the world above, and he knew who he was. There was no amnesia. But he had lost his connection with the memories. He had lost mental continuity. The legacy of the whole of his life—more than twenty years—was suddenly incomplete, inadequate, insane. The facts remained, but all the meaning had somehow drained out of them.

Tears began to ooze from the lachrymal glands in the corner of each eye.

A cockroach, wandering across his face, had to struggle hard to escape when it almost fell into the pit of his open mouth.

22.

Ermold was running. There was, perhaps, just a hint of panic about *his* headlong flight, but it was panic which shared control of him with honest fear and cold rationality. The leaf-bladed dagger which Camlak had flicked into his belly had hurt him badly, but it had done him no permanent damage, if only he could win free to let it heal. The big danger was that running might rip the wound farther and farther open, spout more and more blood from its orifice, and ultimately make it into a mortal blow. No vital organ had been touched, but a hole in the belly was a hole in the belly, and Ermold needed time.

He knew exactly how many men were after him, and he knew that it was no use making any sort of attempt to reduce the odds unless he could get them well and truly strung out. Arrogance assured him that if he could take them one at a time he could dispose of all five. He would have to, if he was to get away. He could hardly hide while he was spilling a trail out of his guts, and the prospect of help arriving was remote indeed.

While he ran, he sustained himself with thoughts of what he could and would do to Huldi and Camlak when he recovered. In order to make those fantasies into fact he *had* to survive, and his indulgence was no mere whim. He was feeding his need, fueling his determination.

Objectively speaking, he had very little chance of getting away. But circumstances are rarely defined objectively. The odds are never what they seem. Probability is a measure of a mechanical universe, not a human one.

He did not attempt to cross the canal. Climbing the low wall would not be difficult, and gaining his own territory would no doubt reduce the advantage enjoyed by the rats, if only in a psychological sense, but he simply dared not dive into the poisoned water with an open wound in him. That *would* be fatal.

He placed his faith in the length of his stride and the innate superiority of man over false man. The innate superiority was a myth, but it was faith that counted and not truth. The length of his stride, however, was an important factor. The Children of the Voice were fast movers, but they were built for short-distance work, not long cross-country chases. While Ermold ran he stayed ahead of his pursuers and gradually, he did begin to string them out. He tired, and they tired, and the battle condensed, temporarily, into a battle of Ermold's wound-affected endurance versus the Shairan warriors' natural endurance.

As the clutching hands of fierce pain and the weakness of lost blood reached out to claim Ermold and put an end to that phase, forcing him to turn and stand, fate intervened.

As he blundered round a cluster of pepper-squab stalks his foot was snagged by a creeper, and he was brought heavily to the ground. The fall jerked the wind out of him and tears blurred his eyes. When he blinked and focused them again he found that his own face was mere inches away from another.

And the other face was made of shiny steel.

23.

Porcel was too far behind Ermold to see him fall, but he slowed down as he came up to the pepper-squabs because of the smell. He knew something was behind the cluster, but he could not for the life of him think what it was.

He did not stop, but he allowed his body to relax into a crouch, with his dagger arm extended before him, ready to tackle anything.

As he came round the corner the steel face was thrust forward into his own. The surprise was just too great. He bounded backwards, hesitated, and then ran.

Ermold dropped Joth's limp body back into the mud and peered through the curtain of creepers after the fleeing warrior. He saw Porcel meet the next man, and the next, and he knew that once all five were gathered together they would pluck up the courage to approach. He glanced down, and saw that Joth was squirming slightly, beginning to recover some vestige of control over his limbs.

Ermold kicked him, but not very hard. "Get up!" he hissed.

But Joth couldn't.

Somewhere, not too far away, a harrowhound howled. Ermold cursed beneath his breath. There were enough hunters abroad without new ones trying to get into the act. But he knew that the harrowhound's nearness might work for him as well as against him. It would worry the Shaira as well, and they wouldn't be keen to split up again.

He reached down and hauled Joth to his feet, shaking him to try and jar some sense into his brain. Finally, Joth could stand. By this time, though, the warriors of Stalhelm were coming forward again.

Ermold shoved Joth forward, steadied him, and then shoved again. Then, without bothering to find out what effect, if any, Joth would have on the advancing Children of the Voice, he turned and ran. The rest had done him little enough good, but he hoped fervently that he would not need the power of his legs much longer.

24.

Joth staggered no more than six paces before slumping forward again. He fell first on to his knees, and then toppled forward face-first into the mud. Moments later, he felt himself being turned over.

His consciousness was still seeping back with tortuous slowness. It was without surprise and without wonder that he looked up at the ring of faces inspecting him.

The creatures were small. Pygmies or dwarfs...perhaps goblins. Their faces were more beast-like than human, but Joth could not for the moment pin a name to the beast. Their noses were large, their eyes small black beads. Their teeth were closely packed inside their mouths. Their ears were tiny and rounded, mounted oddly—too high, too far apart.

He tried to speak, but he was unable to produce any sound other than a low groan which—when he forced it—came out something like a cat's purr.

He gave up the attempt. One of them passed a hand over his face, feeling the metal and the plastic flesh-substitute which, in collaboration, provided the whole structure of his cranium, his eye sockets, his nose and his cheeks. Only his lower jaw and bottom teeth were real—those he had been born with. His eyes were metal orbs, but they functioned as eyes (better than real ones) and they connected to optic nerves which were his own. The olfactory organ, however, was not functional. He had no sense of smell.

"It's a mask," said one of the weird creatures.

"No," said the one who had run hands over his face. "It's real."

Joth realized that they were speaking English. As the faces peered closer he saw that they were covered in sleek gray fur. The fur and the fact that they spoke combined to give him a fleeting sensation of paradox. Then he lost consciousness.

The Shaira argued among themselves for a few moments,

and then came to a decision which might have been motivated more by fear of Ermold than by concern for or interest in Joth. They picked him up by his ankles and his shoulders, and they carried him away in the direction of Stalhelm.

25.

Joth Magner was probably unique among the citizens of the Euchronian Millennium. He was one of the very few members of that society ever to have faced a serious crisis. Not only did he face and survive such a crisis, but he had no choice in the matter. It was forced upon him.

He was probably the only man of his age to have struggled for continued existence over a considerable period of time, and to have taken that struggle as it came, as a matter of course. He was one of very few who had to come to terms with diffi-cult circumstances and physical hardship. Not by choice, but by something akin to necessity.

When Joth was less than a year old a malfunction in a house-hold cyberunit, possibly assisted by some interference at the hands of the older infant Ryan, caused a panel of the unit to explode in his face. He suffered extreme damage to his eyes and his skin was burned away over a considerable area of his scalp and cheeks. Because of the relative softness and flexibility of his skull-bones, and the fact that his brain had not yet grown to fill the skull cavity, Joth's frontal lobes suffered relatively little damage. Nevertheless, it seemed an open-and-shut case so far as the euthanasia board was concerned. Infancy counted against him severely in that he had no voice in the decision and he was considered to be below the threshold of social consciousness.

The strenuous arguments of his father, however, delayed the board in coming to a terminal decision. Carl Magner proved dogged, stubborn and extremely determined. By sheer refusal to entertain any arguments in opposition, and inordinate vehe-mence in putting forward his own opinion over and over again, he prevented the board from making a ruling. While the board was in session, of course, surgeons worked to keep the child alive and to repair the damage done. In the end, with the aid of a clever lawyer, Carl Magner stalled the board long enough for the situation to have changed so materially that the decision went the other way. The baby was permitted to live.

For many months Joth was sightless and quiescent, and even Carl Magner must have wondered whether he had done the right thing in forcing the euthanasia board to bring in a negative verdict. There was a certain amount of public criticism of the board and of Magner's lawyer. Relatively little was said about Magner himself, for whom excuses could obviously be made. But controversy ran high for some time until it was extinguished by the surgeons and a series of educational experts who contrived to prove that the boy was neither physically deficient, nor mentally retarded, nor psychologically aberrant. It was not until Joth was four years old that he finally stilled all arguments as to the rights and wrongs of his specific case by demonstrating his ability to use his artificial eyes effectively, and his brain as well as any child of his own age.

The experience undoubtedly had an effect on Carl Magner, but that was measurable. The effect which it had on Joth, however, was quite unknowable. He grew up to be an intelligent, adaptable and apparently ordinary member of Euchronian Society—ordinary, that is, except for his rather striking physiognomy. But the Euchronian standards of personality assessment were tailored to Euchronian assumptions and criteria. The differences that existed between Joth and other men went somewhat deeper than that. He *was* different, and he knew that he was different. He had paid a price for his individual survival that no other man of the Overworld could evaluate, or even imagine.

Perhaps the accident also made an impression of some kind on Ryan Magner. He was three when the accident happened and only he ever knew whether the explosion was partly his fault or not. But even if not he was at an age to be affected by constant contact with Joth and constant awareness of Joth's difficulties.

The accident which led to the death of Joth's mother had happened some months before the explosion and was totally unconnected with it except insofar as it might have affected Carl Magner's state of mind relative to the euthanasia board. However, it is significant that the family had to endure misfortune that was quite out of proportion with the ordinary flow of life in the Euchronian Millennium.

Whether the incidence of Carl Magner's nightmares had anything to do with the stress placed upon him by either accident or their consequences was not known even to the man himself. It seemed possible, to him and to his doctor.

The adult Joth owed his existence to endurance in conflict. He, in collaboration with others, had fought for life and health throughout his most impressionable years. In a sense, Joth *never* laid down his arms in that struggle to survive. More than any other man of the Overworld, including the most devout Eupsychians, he felt self-contained and somehow detached from his environment. He was not really a misfit, because he adapted perfectly well to his circumstances.

But in different circumstances, the difference between Joth Magner and his contemporaries could, and did, prove crucial.

26.

The close council met in Heres' house, taking advantage of a chamber which was totally isolated from the cybernet. Nothing of what they said went on to any kind of record.

They were discussing a secret which, though not theirs alone, was theirs to protect as they saw fit. Heres was determined to keep the secret. Eliot Rypeck wanted to reveal it to the world. It was a difficult decision, considering that the close council had no theoretical executive power. Theoretically, the close council had no right to exist.

"You're firmly convinced," Rypeck asked Ulicon, "that the origin of Magner's data is his dreams?"

"That's not possible," said Clea Aron. Heres gestured with his hand to keep her quiet.

"I am," said Ulicon.

"And are the dreams accurate?" Rypeck followed up.

"We don't know. We have no up-to-date information. Offhand, I couldn't tell you how to get into the Underworld, though I don't imagine it's difficult. We must send someone to find out, if we can find anyone willing to go. This is something we need to know."

"I'm not so sure that the truth or otherwise of Magner's visions is a point at issue," said Heres. "It's the visions themselves that we ought to be concerned with. One thing we *do* know is that this man has complained of bad dreams over a very long period of time. What we want to know first and foremost is why. Is he immune to the i-minus agent?"

"How do you suggest we test him?" said Ulicon.

"Did you get anything from the doctor?" countered Heres. Ulicon shrugged and shook his head.

"Wait a moment," said Rypeck. "Isn't it more likely that we'll get useful information from Magner himself? We could ask *him* instead of conspiring to get information by all sorts of devious means."

"We can't do that," contributed Acheron Spiro. "Magner's book is a strong attack on the Movement itself. He has set himself up in extreme opposition to us. We can't ask him to explain his dreams because we're worried about them."

"Our hands are tied somewhat in the matter of making inquiries," said Heres. "We can't tell people what we want without letting out the secret we're trying to safeguard with the answers. We have to get the answers without exposing the fact that we're interested."

"This is ridiculous," said Rypeck. "Surely it's clear by now that the i-minus effect is totally and utterly failing to counter the unrest in society. The agent doesn't work—we already know that, or we should. It's time to stop playing games with it and bring it out into the open. If Magner is immune, then maybe others are too, and we have a possible explanation of why the agent hasn't had the effect we've been hoping for. But think of the possibilities which are opened up if Magner *isn't* immune, if the i-minus agent is working perfectly. In that case we might have something entirely new to deal with, and something vitally important. If Magner is mad, we must know *why* he is mad. I don't think we can afford to play this down, to pussyfoot around it, to hesitate and argue and finally fail to reach any meaningful decision. This could be something we ought to know about *now*—something we ought to have known about years ago. And we have to find out."

"Not at the cost of the i-minus plan," said Heres. "You say that things are going badly for us despite i-minus, and I agree with you. But I think that i-minus is all that's standing between us and total breakup. Eleven thousand years have gone into the building of this world and eleven thousand years of responsibility rests on our shoulders."

"That's just my point," interposed Rypeck. "It shouldn't rest on our shoulders."

"But it does," said Heres. "Like it or not, we have charge of the i-minus project as it was handed down to us through thousands of years of closed council. To make the project public is to go half way to destroying it. We simply do not have the *right* to betray the Movement in this way, without full knowledge of what we are doing."

"I say that we are betraying the Movement by keeping the secret," said Rypeck. "The whole concept of a close council is alien to the principles of the Movement, and it's patently ridiculous that six members of the Hegemony, including the Hegemon, should participate in one."

"But nevertheless, a council exists," said Heres, "and we are that council. We cannot dismiss lightly a decision which was taken so long ago and which has served the movement so well for so long. The i-minus effect *has* worked—it worked for generations. Without i-minus, the Euchronian Millennium might not exist. If we cannot cope with the responsibility that we have to deal personally with i-minus then we run the risk of destroying Euchronia."

"All this is a rather haggard argument," said Ulicon. "The question is what we do about Magner. It may turn out that we have to reveal or even abandon i-minus. But let's fight about that when we come to it. And we can't come to it unless we first make every effort to deal with this matter as it lies. We have to make an effort to come to terms with the situation and get ourselves into a position to end it. We want to know three things: Is the i-minus effect still working? Is it working on Magner? Is the input into Magner's dreams an accurate statement of reality? The first is relatively easy to answer, but will take too long. The second is more difficult. If, however, we assume that the answers to the first two questions are both 'yes' then the third becomes absolutely vital. If the first two answers are 'no' then the answer to the third must surely also be 'no.' Doesn't it make sense to mount an expedition to the Underworld at the earliest possible opportunity?"

"I think there's more to consider than that," said Clea Aron. "We shouldn't be obsessed with the i-minus aspect of this affair. It has other implications as well. We mustn't overlook the direct challenge to Euchronia because we're aware of certain deeper issues. Magner wants dealing with purely and simply on political grounds. This plan needs squashing."

"Hardly," said Luel Dascon. "Why should we allow ourselves to look foolish by deigning to take it seriously? I've talked to Abram Ravelvent about this and he assures me that any men in the Underworld will be little better than savage wild animals by now. Much better to produce our own counterproposal to sterilize the Underworld completely—wipe out all its vermin. If we're actually going to send an expedition down there we'll need some sort of reason."

"It would be foolish to take up any such definite stand," said Heres. "I think the opposite angle would be better. Officially, we don't believe a word of what Magner says, but out of the kindness of our hearts we'll send someone down to have a look. We can pretend to have a certain sympathy with him while assuring the world that it's all a fuss over nothing."

"I think Magner could be troublesome," Dascon persisted. "We shouldn't offer him any kind of encouragement."

"Nobody will encourage him," said Heres. "We'll just use him as an excuse to mount our explorations—*all* of our explorations. Luel—you'd better take charge of mounting the expedition. Enzo—keep following up the medical aspect. Find out all you can about Magner's dreams and i-minus effects. Clea—you can handle the media. Acheron and I will handle the Hegemony and the political aspects of the argument. Eliot, you'd better find out what you can about the Underworld from the cybernet. Luel's team will need information as well as equipment."

"You do realize," said Ulicon, "that if there *is* something in the Underworld transmitting ideas into Magner's head, then we might have to face the fact that Earth has two worlds and not one."

There was a brief period of silence.

"I just want to make it clear," Ulicon carried on, "that the implications of Magner's book go a long way beyond our perennial squabbling over the crime rate and the i-minus problem. After eleven thousand years, we may have to confront the fact that the old world didn't die after all, and that something down there might actually pose a threat to us. I say this now because I don't think there's a single one of you has really absorbed this idea, and I think we ought to get used to it. The Underworld *is still there*. Remember that."

27.

Later, Heres ran the whole argument back through his mind, looking for an answer. The important thing, of course, was not to let any part of it get out of hand. Rypeck could be handled— Rypeck had been handled for years. The man lacked a positive side to his character. Argument would never convince him, but it would not be necessary to keep him from acting. Rypeck was not the type to act.

Ulicon, on the other hand, was more difficult to assess. He too was a man who would appeal to the group for justification rather than take any kind of independent initiative, but he would make his appeal on a rather different level. Rypeck dealt in dilute arguments. Ulicon seemed to be dealing in not-so-dilute scare stories.

Any kind of a scare had to be avoided at all costs. That went without saying. But the suggestion of a scare was not necessarily a bad thing. A threat to all helped to unite the group, provided that it could be dealt with in the right way, by the right man. When it came down to it, Rypeck and Ulicon could both be given a role to play in Heres' scheme of things. Ulicon was the man to pose a question, Rypeck to agitate on the basis of the question. Heres, though, was the man to act and answer the question, and by so doing deal with both kinds of opposition. Spiro, Aron and Dascon would thus remain solidly behind him as always, their faith constantly reinforced.

Since the Millennium had begun, the administration represented by Heres and his predecessors had faced no threat to their power except for the Eupsychians, who were really only a fake threat. Under the current régime Eupsychianism had no chance to spread (so Heres believed) and no chance to topple the Movement even if it did. The *real* potential threat was the threat of strife within the Movement itself—such strife as would undoubtedly occur if the matter of the close council and its purpose were to be made public. Heres' first priority was controlling the close council.

Heres regarded the Magner affair, so far as it had gone, as a regrettable inconvenience of strictly temporary concern. Given time, the man would disappear along with his ridiculous ideas. Once the man was out of sight, he would be easy enough to put out of mind. Another of Eliot Rypeck's arguments would go stale, and Enzo Ulicon would abandon his worries about the Underworld. The balance would be restored—another victory for stability. Heres believed, absolutely, in stability.

He also believed quite sincerely in the i-minus effect, which was supposed to control dreams. The fact that Magner was an exception (apparently) to the i-minus rule did not frighten the Hegemon—he believed that every stable situation has room for a handful of misfits, and that stability is enhanced rather than threatened by the visible presence of such wayward factors. Heres, in fact, was quite willing to remain in blissful ignorance of *how* Carl Magner was beating the system in this respect.

Somewhere behind all these attitudes lies the true key to Heres' character. One might describe him as "megaloid"— inferring that he was power-oriented without necessarily being mentally aberrant. In Heres one can definitely see a man who would seek fulfillment through control, control of both environment and situation. This is not to say, however, that Heres had Eupsychian tendencies—quite the reverse. His ideas of control involved a scale of consideration not permitted by a Eupsychian philosophy. He was a lover of pattern and balance, and his efforts were directed to the overall maintenance of pattern rather than to the grasp of personal power of determination.

As Hegemon of the Euchronian Movement and one of the close council Heres sat at the apex of a vast pyramid of executive responsibility. He was not really the most powerful man in the world, and his influence over the vast arena of social action was in many ways the most indirect. But he was the fulcrum of the system. His movements might not cause the biggest ripples, but his ministrations served to damp down most big ripples before they had a chance to grow.

Heres was a vain man—any man with such a degree of self-confidence is necessarily a victim of vanity. But this is one of the so-called "qualities of leadership." Any Hegemon is essentially a vain man. Heres was also an intelligent man, but it might be argued that he was *too* intelligent—that his intelligence was so massive as to prove unwieldy when brought to bear on specific problems. Heres' mind was a mind perennially locked in high gear. Whereas most men despair of the practicality of thinking of two things at once, Heres found difficulty in restraining himself to one. Heres' intelligence lacked small-scale utility. He would throw himself wholeheartedly into the most complex matter and come up with *the* solution of dazzling brilliance. But only the most complex matters. Where smaller things were concerned, he was a fumbler. Like a physical giant who cannot help knocking things over, Heres was a mental giant who was also mentally clumsy.

He was also a dedicated master of the game of Hoh. Hoh, played by novices, can be a competitive affair. Played by experts its competitive aspects are buried in a bewildering range of possibilities. The ideal game of Hoh from the viewpoint of the connoisseur—and far and away the most difficult to play—is the game where *all* the players win. In this kind of game all the players must play with one another as well as against one another, and must unite against the random factors in the game. (When a Eupsychian plays Hoh he almost always tries to end up the sole winner of the game. Such strategies, while perfectly valid under the rules, are frowned upon as simple-minded and contrary to the real spirit of the game by virtually all purists and experts.)

In completing a study of Heres' character it must be noted that he was not a good leader. In many ways he was not a leader at all. He had charisma, and commanded a good deal of respect, but he was not very efficient. He was clever—but like a driver who takes his corners late he needed to be clever. He was not really good because he was not really safe. The Magner affair illustrates this. While others were worrying Heres was merely observing. It would not occur to him to act decisively at this stage. He had every confidence that if things got worse he could bring off a mental riposte of startling elegance, but the fact remains that if another man were in control the problem might not have been allowed to develop in the way it did. Many men close to him were aware of this failing in the Hegemon's character, but there was nothing, really, that they could do about it.

Except worry.

28.

Huldi's reception in Stalhelm was a poor one. The Children of the Voice, especially those who could be termed neighbors of Ermold, harbored no affection whatsoever for the Men Without Souls, despite the fact that some of the things which enriched their lives came from Walgo.

When Camlak brought her back, not as a captive for ransom but as a fugitive seeking protection, the women of the village were amazed, if not appalled. The women had lived long by Yami's ways, which were hard ways. Life as they knew it tended to be ruled by the principle: if in doubt—kill. Camlak made it known that Huldi had killed one of Walgo's fighting men, and that she hated Ermold as virulently as any Shairan, but those were not reasons which the women would accept as sufficient to permit Huldi the freedom of Stalhelm. Hellkin were welcome enough in the village, and there had been times when Men Without Souls passed freely in and out of the gate—as they undoubtedly did in the villages of western Shairn. But the women were ruled by memory and by habit, and Camlak's choice did not rest easily with them. Camlak had always been something of an enigma.

The Old Man's son installed Huldi in his own house when it was clear that she would not be accommodated elsewhere.

There she was made welcome, after a fashion, by Camlak's daughter (by the woman Xyli) Nita. Camlak's present woman, Sada, objected to the intrusion in no uncertain terms, but dared not show her displeasure in full measure while Camlak was present. Eventually, however, Camlak went to confer with Yami and the elders in the long house, and some of the spite was allowed out.

After a few insults Sada left to work and to talk with the other village women, but Nita stayed. She was old enough now to work, and should, perhaps, have been out in the fields, but she enjoyed a certain latitude by virtue of being kin to the Old Man.

Nita was fascinated by Huldi. In the present troubled times she had never actually seen a woman of the Soulless Ones. She had never been close to a living Man at all, though she had seen plenty of warriors' heads brought home to adorn the skull-gate. She was amazed to discover how tall the stranger was. One got no real idea of size from a distance (and none at all from skulls). She could not imagine that the girl really needed so much body to support a head which did not seem unduly massive.

Nita had heard from the women that the inhabitants of Walgo were child-eating giants only one step removed from the ultimately horrifying Ahrima, but Nita had always been ready to discredit such talk because it lacked Camlak's endorsement. Everyone knew that the old women lied about almost everything. The sheer size of Huldi was enough to keep her suspicions awake in some degree, but for the most part Nita's attitude to the newcomer was not unfriendly.

Huldi squatted in a corner when Camlak left her, ready to defend herself if necessary, but she relaxed once Sada had gone, and discovered that she was very tired. The elation which had followed her success in winning free of Ermold was evaporated by now, and she was afraid. It was all very well to think of running away to Shairn while Ermold had her on the end of a leash, but the fact was something else entirely. She was alone now, with no idea of what she was or what was going to happen to her. She had to pin her faith on Camlak because there was no alternative, but she could not possibly know the degree to which that faith might or might not be justified. The only refuge from fear which was immediately available was sleep, and to sleep she went, while Nita sat and played with a handful of sticks in the opposite corner of the room.

Later, Yami came in—without Camlak—to look at her. No sooner had he crossed the threshold than Sada was behind him.

"You should kill her," said Sada.

Yami did not reply, but simply stood there, looking at the girl with his pale, rheumy eyes. Sada dared to let loose a short, hissing sound which expressed something of her contempt for the man who was old in fact as well as in title. It was time that he was replaced. She had hoped Camlak would do it, but by now she was half-convinced that Camlak would not even if he could. She was disillusioned, and felt betrayed by circumstance. She had grown to hate Camlak, considering him only half a man. Camlak tolerated her anyway, which made her conviction all the stronger.

Yami looked at Huldi, and he wondered. He did not understand. He had reared Camlak to be a leader, and he had failed—or so he believed. Perhaps he had been half-hearted in his determination. No man looks forward to being deposed by his son, no matter how deep his faith in the way the world works, and in the ultimate inevitability and lightness of that way.

"I ought to kill her myself," muttered Sada.

Yami laughed at her derisively. He did not bother to turn and face her.

"Well?" said Sada. "What has he brought her here for?"

"To be a wife instead of you," said Yami coldly. The suggestion was mildly obscene.

"He's mad enough," she mumbled. "Mad enough to take a beast to his bed."

"Shut up," said the Old Man.

"I'll see her dead," Sada promised herself, audibly. "I'll see her dead."

Yami turned to spit at her. "You only kill babies," he said. "You see them *all* dead."

Then he turned on his heel and went to the long house. Sada watched him go, with a savage glare in her eyes. She had borne her children, but they were all dead. Only one of Camlak's children lived, and that was his by another woman. She had killed no child—to think of such a thing was impossible. It was the deadliest insult Yami could throw. Yami blamed it all on her. She blamed Camlak. A man should have more than one child, and no woman should die childless.

Sada grabbed Nita by the scruff of the neck and shoved her out of the house, telling her to go to work. She might have attacked Huldi then, or even fulfilled her threat of murder while fury blinded her to the consequences. But she was distracted by something which was happening outside. There was a commotion which grew quickly. Porcel and the others were coming back. At the thought that they might have Ermold's head Sada rushed out to join the crowd.

29.

"Is it true," Nita asked Huldi, "that you have no Soul?"

Huldi was busy making a meal of the scraps which had been left after Camlak had gone back to the long house. She had been given a share in the meal but she thought it wise to guard against the future. She looked up at the shadowed form of the girl-child, not sure that she should answer, or even that she *could* answer.

"Is it true?" persisted Nita.

"No," said Huldi, not knowing whether it was truth or lie, and not caring greatly.

"Why do we call you Men Without Souls?" asked Nita.

"*We* don't," countered Huldi.

"Everyone else does," claimed the child.

"They don't," Huldi contradicted her flatly.

Nita thought that there was no point in quoting instances. She was obviously not on the right track. "What do you call yourselves?" she asked, instead.

"Men," said Huldi, shortly.

Nita pondered this revelation for a few moments. "What do you call us?" she asked. "We're men, but we call ourselves Children of the Voice."

"You're Rats," said Huldi.

"Why?" asked Nita.

It was an unanswerable question, and it threw Huldi out of her stride for a moment while she tried to examine the possibility of finding an answer. She was tempted to say: It's what you are, but that didn't seem to advance the argument at all. In addition, to call someone a Rat was the ultimate insult in Walgo. Perhaps she should be more careful and less honest.

"I don't know," she said, finally.

"What's your name?" inquired Nita.

"Huldi."

"Why did you come here?"

"There was nowhere else to go."

"Are you going to stay?"

"I don't know."

Nita considered this series of answers with all due serious-ness, and decided that they were not really adequate. She tried to figure out a way of demanding a better answer, but couldn't find one. Then Huldi went on.

"I wanted to get away," she said. "They would have killed me. I tried to kill Ermold. I would have killed him, if I could. I wanted to get away from him. I don't know what I can do now. I can't live on my own."

"You could," said Nita.

"No." Huldi shook her head.

Nita considered further, and decided that she had had enough of questions and answers.

"I'm going out," she said. "I want to know what's happening in the long house. They have a man with no face, and they don't know what to do. Yami will kill him, but I don't know how."

Huldi simply did not know how to react to this information, so she did not. She simply watched Nita go out of the house. Then she moved back into her corner, wondering what to do— and what alternatives might be before her.

30.

Abram Ravelvent came to a decision.

Carl Magner was important. Carl Magner was not so ridicu-lous as had been supposed.

Ravelvent found a certain amount of sense in *The Marriage*

of Heaven and Hell. He still did not believe in it, but he discovered a certain attractiveness in its ideas. On top of that, it was obvious that something was brewing. He had been asked for advice by members of the Hegemony and by Alwyn Ballow. People were taking sides in the Magner affair.

Ravelvent decided that he was on Magner's side if he was on anybody's. As a man of science—a man without prejudice—he felt no disposition to take the side of Heaven rather than that of Hell. Quite the reverse, in fact. To take the bad end of the case *looked* more objective. It was definitely more promising, from the point of view of wringing out some good argument.

The criteria by which Ravelvent selected his stand may sound somewhat vague—that is because they were somewhat vague in his own mind—but they were sufficient to commit him. He looked upon the whole affair as an academic exercise. Having made up his mind what he was going to prove he set about gathering evidence in a thoroughly scientific manner, by painstaking research. He had no intention whatsoever of going down into the Underworld himself but he offered to lend his advice and his moral support to the expedition which was being mounted.

Ravelvent borrowed Magner's arguments and embroidered them. He disentangled them and reset them into a pattern which was largely his own. He shored up a few of the weak spots with speculative logic and added a few details to help round out the picture. Then he threw his weight into the gathering controversy. It was not too difficult for a man of his argumentative caliber to convince others that there might be something in Magner's book.

There were half a dozen more like Ravelvent. Together, they managed to form a rallying point for all those who had some kind of sympathy for Magner. The Eupsychians flocked to the banner in droves, eager to recruit any idea which might be magnified into a thorn to prick the Movement. There was hardly one of the principal supporters of Magner's cause who lent any real credence to his allegations, let alone any real conviction to his conclusions, but the cause grew anyway. Magner was uplifted—and exposed.

The world, at this stage, was only playing a game. But it meant a lot more than that to Magner. Magner stood to suffer from the way the game went. He had already suffered a great deal. The pressure on him was on a totally different order to anything else in the game. For him, as for his faceless son, it was a game of life and death.

31.

Randal Harkanter was the man who was asked to lead the descent into the Underworld. He was by no means Heres' number-one choice—in fact, his selection represented a certain desperation in the whole matter of selection. Everybody was suddenly interested in the Underworld, but nobody wanted to go. Who could blame them?

Luel Dascon, the Hegemon's right-hand man, finally decided that Harkanter was the only reasonable prospect, and approached him.

Harkanter was a big man, over six feet tall, with a strong liking for games of a rather more primitive kind than were popular in the society of Euchronia's Millennium. Harkanter was a fierce competitor, with the attitude of a hunter. At fifty years of age he was starting what could well be a very long prime of life.

He was implicitly Eupsychian in his approach to life, but he was in no way politically inclined. Insofar as the Eupsychians were organized into a form of political opposition he despised them utterly. He was a strong-minded man who believed that he could get what he wanted, and who believed that anyone who couldn't get what they wanted was unworthy of his attention. He had no time for philosophical arguments about the form of society. His ideas and needs were far more basic.

He was a complete misfit.

"A situation has arisen," Dascon told him, "which opens up some rather interesting possibilities. Interesting to us, and to you, in rather...er...different ways. The question concerns the Underworld."

Harkanter was surprised. Dascon was not surprised by Harkanter's surprise. Harkanter was not the sort of man to pay any attention to matters like the Magner affair. Harkanter had probably never heard of Carl Magner, or *The Marriage of Heaven and Hell*. Or William Blake, for that matter.

"So?" said Harkanter.

"It has been claimed that there are human beings still living on the old surface," said Dascon.

"Rubbish," said Harkanter, positively.

"That is what needs to be ascertained. The question has been raised, and no matter how ludicrous it may seem, we need direct evidence to answer it. It has been suggested that the Overworld be opened to allow some kind of commerce between the platform and the surface. The idea is causing speculation. We need facts to counter that speculation."

"What's it to me?" Harkanter wanted to know.

"We need a man to lead an exploratory party into the Underworld. It's a job for which few enough men have the qualifications. Everyone's interested, but nobody wants to take the trouble to find out."

"Send a contingent of police," said Harkanter.

"It's not a police job. The police are no more qualified than anyone else. We have half a dozen scientists whose appetite for facts is strong enough to reconcile them to the idea of taking a look down there, but they'll need someone to look after them—someone they can trust to make sure they come to no harm. You qualify. I think you'll find the experience stimulating."

"Why don't you just stamp on the whole argument?" asked Harkanter. "Issue a flat statement that no life exists down there."

"We can't," said Dascon.

"Too many people want to argue. The Eupsychians?"

"Partly. But we *do* want to know the truth ourselves. It might be important."

Harkanter laughed. "You want *me* to help you squash some Eupsychian propaganda."

"Why not?"

The big man shrugged.

"You are interested?" said Dascon tentatively.

"So are you," retorted Harkanter, "but there's nobody in the Hegemony going to spend a fortnight sightseeing in the sewers. Why should I?"

Dascon smiled politely. "It's your kind of challenge, Randal. Isn't it? Wouldn't you envy anyone else who got this particular patch of limelight? The first expedition into the nether world for...what?...five thousand years? Perhaps more. Certainly, it will involve contact with a certain amount of dirt—but you've always despised people who won't dirty their hands. It may involve a certain amount of *danger*—but you can handle yourself and you're proud of the fact. There isn't that much opportunity for this kind of excitement nowadays...." Dascon allowed the sentence to fade out gracefully, prompting Harkanter's imagination to take up the thread of the argument.

It already had.

"There's not a lot of excitement to be found grubbing around in the sewers," said Harkanter. "I don't go out to find excitement: I go out to make it"

"Will you do it?" asked Dascon, easily, confident that Harkanter was well and truly hooked by now.

"I'll do it," said the big man. "I'll get some stuff together and provide a couple of extra hands to help keep your tame scientists safe from the crocodiles, or whatever. I guess I'm a fool but if it's going to be done it might as well be me. It'll be dark down there, I suppose?"

Dascon shrugged elegantly. "I would imagine so," he said. His voice sounded suddenly distant. He had said what he had to say. After he had closed the circuit he took out a handkerchief and wiped the palms of his hands. His smile had vanished without trace.

32.

There was a long period of sickness and delirium. Joth lay on a bed of straw in the best room in Camlak's house. Camlak had saved him, Camlak accepted responsibility for him. Joth did not know how close he had come to death in the long house.

Even as it was, he was close enough to death. His mind was rarely in possession of his brain for more than a few minutes. He had fever after fever, and both Nita and Huldi spent long hours by his side trying to cool him. Sada would not help. She no longer lived in Camlak's house.

They fed him broth made from gray meat and the flesh of various beasts. At first his stomach rejected them all, and whatever they made him swallow he would instantly vomit back. But they made him take water to replace what he sweated off, and gradually they were able to enrich the water with some kind of sustenance. The period of adjustment was long, but in due time Joth became accustomed to the food of the Underworld and he recovered from those diseases which took hold of him. Occasionally he would speak or cry out, and there were many occasions when tears would flood from his eyes as he sobbed helplessly. In the early time his skin swelled and broke out into rashes perpetually as his exposure to alien proteins caused reactions in his flesh.

Gradually, however, the sharp smell which marked his body as alien dwindled and was lost, and his body adapted to the new environment.

The adaptation of his mind made some progress over the same period, but long after he was taking food regularly and sleeping without fever his consciousness retained the alien-ness that his body had rejected.

The time was hard for Camlak, Huldi and Nita, because what they were doing was, in a sense, just as alien as Joth. It was not the way that life was lived among the Children of the Voice. It was not Yami's way. In a different time, perhaps Camlak would not have been given the opportunity to defy convention and opinion, but Yami was old and ageing faster all the time.

But if it was hard for Camlak to bring something alien into his world, it was ten times as hard for Joth to accept that he had come into that world. He found it difficult to locate himself, almost impossible to rediscover himself. Physiologically, he only had to be rehabituated. Mentally—perhaps spiritually—he had to be reshaped.

Joth was born again in Stalhelm. The world of Euchronia's Millennium, in which he had lived for more than twenty years, faded away as if it had been a dream. It retreated into his memory so far that it became almost unreal. It remained *his* world, insofar as he knew he had come from there, and it remained his insofar as he was determined that he should return to it if he could, but as a real and living world it was largely replaced by a whole new set of precepts and contexts.

The hold which Joth had on his own world—and the hold which it had on him—were naturally slight and superficial. Joth had no instincts.

He was lost, for a time, inside himself. He spent a period of time in nowhere. The people who tended him understood and accepted that, and they allowed him to come back in his own time. The people of the Underworld did not count, weigh and trade in time as did the people of Heaven, who were ruled by the metrication of days and nights. They had a better understanding of time and a more amicable relationship with it than did the people of the Overworld.

When Joth awoke, in the real sense of the word, he found himself occupied by fear. Not panic, but fear. He had found himself a balance. For a long time—subjective time—after his rebirth, Joth could find nothing in his past but insanity. But he was in something of a privileged position. He did know what a nightmare was. He had a label to apply, and a context into which his experiences could be set. It was a good start.

He remembered Ermold—just—but could make no sense of that particular encounter. He remembered the warriors finding and carrying him, too, and could make no sense of that either. But he could also remember Huldi and Nita and Camlak feeding him, tending him, cleaning him and cooling him. This he could make sense of. This he understood. These three individual beings he accepted as his friends, his relatives, his kindred of the new birth. He began to love them without being conscious of the fact, and he continued to love them likewise.

Two worlds met by Joth's bedside, and became caught up with one another.

When Joth finally knew for sure that he was alive, awake and real, Nita was beside him. He looked at her, trying to decide exactly what manner of being she might be. A dwarf. A child of a dwarf-people. A face like an animal, but too human to be anything but the face of a man—a girl, a child.

He searched his mind for something to say, and could find absolutely nothing. He knew that his failure must be written in his face, along with his fear. He looked around, and saw that they were alone in a small room. One lamp burned on a bracket in the wall. The walls seemed to be made of clay or crude plaster, but here and there the surface had crumbled to reveal the infrastructure, which consisted of bricks and square stones cemented together. The ceiling—also, presumably, the roof—slanted gently away from him, and was made of wood with the cracks sealed by the same plaster/clay.

He sighed and relaxed, letting his head sink back. The girl looked at him curiously, and reached out a hand to touch him. His face—the flesh beneath the metal hood—was hot, but not wet. There was sweat on his neck, though.

"The face," she murmured, trying to prompt him to speak.

"I was hurt," he said. "They repaired me. A long time ago."

She accepted that. "The eyes," she said, very quietly. "The eyes can see. But they are only bowls of metal. Metal lids, metal eyes."

"Yes," he said, finding words and glad of the opportunity to use them. "They replaced my eyes. The eyes work well. Better than real eyes." He whispered, as she did, not sure whether it was necessary.

"Better than mine?" she asked. Her eyes were small, wide-set but mobile and keen.

"Perhaps," he said.

"Your chin," she said. "Your ears, your head."

"Some is plastic flesh, not metal," he said. "They did what they could. But the plastic needs a base of real flesh. Where they had to cut to the bone, they had to use metal. The rest of me is real. All save a few scars of plastic. Quite human."

"Are there men in your world who are all metal?" she asked.

He wanted to answer, to reinforce his friendship for the child, but he was by no means sure what answer to give. There were robots in the old world—Euchronia's world—but were they men, by her definition? He decided not, in the end. The robots were never wholly humanoid.

"No," he said. "All men are flesh and blood. I was hurt. I have only been repaired. You understand? The top of my face was burned away."

She shook her head. "We don't repair men," she said. "Who burned you?"

"No one," he told her. He felt no impulse to laugh at her assumption that he had been burned deliberately. He knew that the question was serious. "It was an accident," he explained.

She said nothing for a few moments, looking pensive.

Then she said: "I knew, really."

"What?" he asked.

"That the men of the world above aren't made of metal. Some of the children have been saying so. The women say so. And worse things. It's the old women making up things. I knew better. All the time."

Again, no impulse to laugh. Had this been a human child...a child of the Overworld.... But it *was* a human child, though not of the Overworld. Joth felt a moment of confusion. Was it...she?... human? Of course, he decided. But in that case, what, precisely, did the word "human" mean?

"How did you know?" he asked. He was not humoring her.

He wanted to know. She could help him find out...everything....
She could be his teacher.

"I can read," she said. She said it flatly, not proudly. It was
not a boast. Reading, to her, was part of the pattern of life. She
could read, therefore she knew. Others, presumably, were not so
fortunate.

"Burstone," he murmured. "He brings you books. In the suitcase. That's what he was carrying. But why?"

She didn't reply. She didn't know what he was talking about.

He knew that he ought to begin to question her, to begin the
long business of learning about his new world, but he was tired,
and he hardly knew where to start. And he was still afraid.
Very much afraid. His fear inhibited clear thinking. There was
another priority, above that of learning. He had to know whether
there was a way out, a way back. If not....

He faced the thought of death. Ryan had died in the
Underworld. Somewhere.

He said: "The lights in the sky...," and paused. He had spoken
loudly. She looked around quickly.

"We have no sky," she said, swiftly, as though time might be
running short. "We have a roof. Some of them call it the sky, but
they cannot read. The stars are set in the roof. The roof of the
world. The sky is beyond that. I do not know how far." There
was a dullness, almost a sadness, in the words as she spoke
them.

He tried hard to see the special significance in what she said,
but he could not.

"The lights in the roof," he said. "Do they always shine?"

"Always," she said.

"They have always been there?" he asked.

"Always," she said, patiently.

"We didn't know," he muttered, feeling that some kind of
explanation was due. "I didn't believe him. I didn't really believe
in the stars. But he was right."

Suddenly, before his mind had time to frame another question, she was gone. She had heard something outside. He looked

at the curtain which hung over the doorway, which stirred slightly after her withdrawal.

He waited. He lay quite still. Wondering. Helpless.

33.

Porcel was counting his blessings. There didn't seem to be very many. But time was on his side. He had not been forgiven for bringing back Joth instead of Ermold's head, and naturally enough the rumor that he had been frightened out of his wits by his first sight of the man with the metal face had been aired all over the village. But it would die, given time.

Porcel had ambition. He wanted to be Old Man. He didn't think much of Camlak's chances, and in open competition he had a better chance than most of imposing his will. He was a strong man, and a fierce fighter. The Communion of Souls was about due—an attack by Ermold was expected any time. So Porcel was estimating his chances, and thinking of ways to improve them. He had the time to think. Camlak was not in the village, nor were the warriors, for the most part. They were out in the fields, planning and organizing defenses. He had been detailed to stand guard at the long house. Apart from a handful of warriors at the gate there were only women and elders and children within the wall.

Porcel knew that there was no point in standing guard at the long house. It was a purely ceremonial duty. Hence he was bored, and thinking hard. Could he provoke a fight with Camlak? Could he arrange things so that Camlak would *have* to fight him, and on his own terms?

While he was thinking, he saw Nita slip through the skull-gate and make for Camlak's house. He watched her, knowing that she was going to the man with the metal face. Porcel had decided that he hated the man with the metal face, and that it would have been sensible to have lopped off his head while the opportunity was there. He would hardly have been able to claim much credit for lopping a head of a quiescent body, but to have settled the matter there and then would have meant that subsequent trouble could have been avoided entirely. Yami was at odds with his son for taking the alien in, but he was also at odds with Porcel for having brought him in in the first place.

Porcel decided that he would take Nita as a wife. Such a marriage would be desirable if he were to become Old Man, as some sense of kinship between rulers seemed proper. In addition, Camlak would hate the idea and Porcel would enjoy taking some of his hatred for Camlak out on the child. Further to these very good reasons was the ambition of simple carnal lust.

The warrior's eyes dwelt on the doorway to Camlak's house while these thoughts ran round his idle mind, and he began to feel resentment and determination rise within him.

Sada passed him by then, and shot him a quick glance as she did so. She muttered something about there not being a man left in the village, maliciously, just loud enough for him to catch the general drift of her meaning. He lost his temper and stepped quickly toward her. Sada ran away, past Camlak's house and in between two others. Rather than run to catch up with her, Porcel kept walking, straight through Camlak's threshold and into his house. The woman Ayria was there, having taken over the household duties from the disespoused Sada. She looked up in surprise as Porcel strode in.

She ducked the first blow he threw, but was too completely off her guard to dodge the second—a wild, backhanded smash with no real malicious intent but quite some power. It caught the side of her head and knocked her over. She whimpered, completely bewildered by the warrior's behaviour.

Porcel paused, realizing that there was no point in taking out his vindictiveness on Ayria, who had done no one any harm, but the rage of his bitterness carried him away for a few moments more. He looked around, clenching his fist convulsively. Nita came out of the back room to find out what was happening.

She tried to get round Porcel to the door and failed. He grabbed her and lifted her off the ground, his eyes flaring suddenly as his anger found a real target. He lost all thought of consequence and gave way to the full force of his inner fury. He hurled the child to the ground, flat on her back, and ripped her ragged skirt apart. She had no other garment underneath.

Porcel dropped heavily on top of her, pinning her securely before reaching down to dispose of his own skirt.

Ayria backed away into a corner, totally bewildered and settled into immobility, watching without understanding.

But someone understood. Sada, curious as to why Porcel had gone into Camlak's house, had come back to find out. She lifted a corner of the cloth which covered the door and began to laugh. She was delighted by the thought of what was happening.

Nita could not find the breath to scream. The sudden and unexpected assault had left her completely winded. The weight of Porcel's body crushing her seemed to preclude the possibility of any air even reaching her lungs again, and she was convinced that she was dying. She felt Porcel fumbling at her groin but she experienced no pain at all as he tried to thrust into her. All the pain was locked into her chest and head, and she was terror-stricken because it would not come out and let her draw breath.

Even when Porcel's weight was summarily snatched away she could not suck air into her lungs and she had no idea of what was happening. She was simply alone with her terror.

Joth kicked Porcel clear out of the door, sending Sada bounding backwards out of the way. He followed up, and kicked the warrior again, as hard as he could. He felt a quick wave of satisfaction as the blow had similarly spectacular results. Joth weighed more than twice as much as Porcel, and he had long legs. He was not back to peak fitness by any means, but he had power enough.

By the time Porcel realized what was happening to him he was half naked and sprawling in the mud halfway back to the portal of the long house. The first time he tried to rise he slipped and fell back into the glutinous filth of the street At first, he realized only that he had been hit and hit hard, and his actions were purely reflexive. But then he realized who had hit him, and how.

He also realized that he was in full view of half the village. Sada was whooping and an audience would not be long in gathering.

He made a noise that was pure animal, and reached for his weapon. Joth hung back momentarily, unsure of himself, and Porcel found the time to come to his feet and take the long knife from its scabbard. While Joth still hesitated, the warrior launched himself murderously into the attack.

Joth had not expected the little man he had kicked so effectively to transform himself into a ferocious—and very fearsome—beast with a vicious instrument of murder and a clear intention of using it.

In the split second that Joth saw Porcel coming he remembered that he was still exhausted, very stiff, and had never indulged in any form of violence in the whole of his active life.

He would have been stone dead within a second if Porcel had not been so completely driven by mad hatred. The warrior was far, far faster than the man from the world above, and Joth's clumsy attempt to get out of the way would have availed him nothing if Porcel had not been so utterly determined to ram home his point with every last vestige of strength he could muster.

But sheer inertia carried Porcel's point a fraction of an inch past Joth's swerving waist. The same inertia took Porcel the way of the blade.

The two bodies collided, but Joth remained unhurt and more or less unmoved. The relative masses of the two men made it inevitable that it was Porcel who was thrown off balance to sprawl once again in the dirt. Joth won a precious second or so to scramble away. He made the best possible use of it.

But there was no possibility of escape. Joth couldn't run. Porcel whirled as he rolled right back to the doorway of Camlak's house, and then he stopped deliberately, allowing himself the luxury of two seconds to collect himself and to control and discipline his anger. He decided in that brief space of time exactly how he was going to begin carving Joth into small slices.

There was one instant in which Joth met his murderer's eyes, and read all the malice and the hate therein. Somewhere at the back of his mind he noted, with some wonder, the intense humanness of Porcel's registered emotions.

Then Porcel's mind went absolutely blank. He collapsed silently in a ragged heap. He fell on top of his knife, but it did not pierce him.

Huldi stepped out of the doorway, still holding the cooking pot she had hit him with. She looked round, fearfully, at the circle of eager faces.

Sada was laughing.

34.

Eliot Rypeck was a small, excitable man with an unusual combination of mental proclivities. On the one hand he was a man who could pay excessive attention to trivia (something of a collector's quirk) and on the other he was one of the few men who had a genuine understanding of the way in which man and the cybernet were potentially capable of establishing a quasi-symbiotic collaborative relationship within the context of mechanized society. Because of this, he was something of a two-sided coin. His determined opposition to the perpetuation of the i-minus project beyond the Plan and into the Millennial society itself reflects the *second* side of the coin—the basis of this particular conviction was the belief that man should be allowed full scope to adapt himself wholly to the new environment of the cybernet. While the instinct-suppressor was in use, he believed that this could not be achieved.

Rypeck was not expert in any particular field, but with respect to any specific topic which happened to attract his attention he was capable of very rapidly picking out significant factors and gaining a good working understanding of it. His affinity with the cybernet was only a good working relationship after this fashion, but by the standards of the early Millennium it was remarkable.

Heres and Rypeck were natural enemies to some extent The form of their personalities was such that they clashed inevitably over method and manner. Rypeck was an older man than Heres, and became a member of the close council before Heres joined it. Heres would not have permitted a man like Rypeck to be coopted into the council once he became Hegemon, but once a secret is shared, there is no way of taking it back. A member of the close council, once inducted, was a member for life.

It might be argued that it was Rypeck who should have been Hegemon and not Heres. Again, this reflects the difference between their characters. Rypeck would have been a more efficient administrator, but it was Heres who commanded the following. In fact, had their positions been reversed both Rypeck and Heres would probably have found the situation intolerable.

Like Heres, Rypeck was an excellent Hoh player. His basic assumptions and strategies were different, but he worked toward similar ends, and his play was only marginally less masterful than the Hegemon's. Hoh provided an important touching point for their minds and personalities. It enabled them to get along together. Hoh was important in the lives of both men.

35.

"I have to confess," said Rypeck, "that I'm frightened."

Heres regarded the image in his screen soberly. Though there was no animosity in his expression he could not keep it out of his voice.

"There's no need for melodrama," he said.

"I am *frightened*," insisted Rypeck, "by the extent of our ignorance."

"Well then," said Heres, "I suggest you set about alleviating some of that ignorance by telling me what you're talking about."

"I'm talking about dependence on the cybernet," said Rypeck. "Not the old, old argument about where would we all be if the net stopped working—I'm talking about a different *kind* of dependence altogether.

"Quite apart from its operational functions the cybernet provides us with a central data storage system. That, of course, is one function that the cybernet is uniquely equipped to handle. It is at this point that we ought to see the perfect partnership of man and machine. The machine provides data storage, sorting and processing facilities while the man provides creative thought and purpose.

"You know all about the controversies concerning machine intelligence and the possibility of the machine's being able to provide the human element of the partnership itself. But you've probably not considered an alternative problem."

"Get to the point," said Heres.

"The point is," said Rypeck, "that instead of worrying about one element in the partnership crossing the gap and fulfilling all functions by itself, we ought to be worrying about the gap becoming so wide that the functions cannot be fulfilled at all."

"You don't make sense," said Heres, drumming his fingers on the console of his desk unit.

"Let me put it this way," said Rypeck. "The machine isn't duplicating human functions—but the human is *failing* to duplicate, in any meaningful degree, the machine functions. We are becoming too specialized as providers of creative thought and purpose. The cybernet provides us with a supremely efficient data store, but in order to use that store we must retain some sort of idea of what it contains and what processes may be used in order to exploit it properly. The cybernet is infallible. It never forgets. But this does not mean that *we* can forget everything we ever knew. In order to use the data in the net we have to know it is there. The partnership cannot work if neither element in it has any conception of what the other can contribute. The gap becomes uncrossable.

"Because we rely on the cybernet to be our memory we have become an ignorant people. Not only that, but we do not even realize that we are ignorant. Because the cybernet knows everything, we consider that we do too. But what use is information in the cybernet if we do not know it is there, and would not know its relevance if we did?"

"Eliot," said Heres, "I'm busy. Did you call me to argue about a purely theoretical point or have you actually got something to say?"

Rypeck sighed. "Yes," he said, "I have something to say. I want to say that we are ignorant, and that our ignorance frightens me. But as that's not what you want to hear I'll tell you some other things instead.

"I've been trying to find out what we know about the Underworld. I expected to find that we know virtually nothing. I never gave a moment's thought to the Underworld until this matter came up. I assumed it had been ignored ever since the platform was completed. I was wrong. There is a good deal of information about the Underworld in the net. Some of it is very disturbing information.

"Firstly, there is life in the Underworld. Secondly, it isn't absolutely confined there. Spores from the Underworld plant kingdom and microfauna of all kinds flow constantly into the lower regions of our own world. The machines at the lower levels are equipped to deal with this constant invasion and do so most effectively. Almost nothing is manifest on the surface itself because these organisms are not equipped to compete effectively with surface organisms. But a number of species now established on the surface undoubtedly originated in the Underworld after the separation. There are no less than forty different kinds of automatic devices specifically designed to cope with the invasion of Underworld organisms in the lower levels. They are efficient. Within limits.

"The Underworld is illuminated by several millions of electric lights set in the ceiling of that world—on the underside of the floors of our lowest levels. Their power consumption is not great compared to the power consumption of our own lighting facilities, but it is significant. Thus there are several facts for you to think about. The Underworld is alive, and it is alive—at least in part—because we keep it alive. It is not completely separate from us and it never has been. Enzo told us all at the close council meeting to remember the Underworld—to remember that the world the Movement abandoned is still there. I say that remembering is not enough. We should never have forgotten the Underworld.

"Rafael, I have been working on this for a matter of days. What else is there that I ought to know? What else is there in the net that I might be able to find—if I knew what to look for? This is more important than the Magner affair. It's more important even than the Underworld. We haven't *begun* to count the cost of the eleven thousand years of the Plan, in terms of knowledge which we have lost and which we are making almost no effort to recover. We're as innocent as newborn children, Rafael, can't you understand that?"

"You're getting upset about nothing," said Heres flatly. "I advise you to think about it for a while. What's the point in coming to me with a lot of garbled nonsense like that? We need the information about the Underworld now, and it's there to be recovered. All you have to do is recover it. Just get the facts, and forget the rest."

"That's just the trouble," said Rypeck. "We have forgotten the rest."

Heres made a gesture of annoyance and switched off the screen.

36.

Rypeck was not the only one who went digging for information in the cybernet and found more than he bargained for. Alwyn Ballow conducted some research for Yvon Emerich, preparatory to exposing Magner to the cameras. And Abram Ravelvent went in search of knowledge partly for its own sake and partly for the benefit of Harkanter's expedition, which was getting together very slowly and in no apparent hurry.

The degree of success which they enjoyed in searching out facts was various. Ballow did not get very far, but he did manage to find out about the lights. Ravelvent found out about the lights early on in his study and was inspired to investigate the flow of energy from Overworld to Underworld in rather more detail. In this matter he found a great deal more than he bargained for. A study of the energy budget over the Overworld covering a period of ten or a hundred years would probably have told him nothing. But Ravelvent, unlike Rypeck and Ballow, was pursuing a rather broader picture of the possible basis on which life in the Underworld subsisted. He dealt in thousands of years. With the calculative facilities of the cybernet there was no reason why he should not. Over a thousand years, even the tiniest discrepancies show up. And once he had located one discrepancy he began to locate more, and more.

Ultimately, he was forced to the quite fantastic conclusion that export from the Overworld to the Underworld was not merely a matter of light energy and waste products. A steady trickle of materials of many kinds had been working its way into the Underworld for years. Not only the years of the Millennial society, but also the many long years of the Plan. In the days when every last ton of usable metal and every last scrap of paper should have been under strict control no less than in the days of present affluence there had been a steady drain of material into the world below. Manufactured goods had been continually exported, albeit on a microscopic scale, consistently since the day the platform was complete. Someone was—and had been for a very long time—supplying the Underworld with metal and with paper and with plastic. Weapons, tools and books.

Ravelvent was forced to conclude that it was the Movement itself which was responsible. There seemed to be no alternative. But whoever was directing the supply, it was obvious that the machines of the Overworld were supporting not one world, but two.

37.

Porcel woke up with a sick headache. He was somewhat surprised to find that he was still alive. Had Camlak arrived back while he was unconscious, there was every chance that he might not have been. But Camlak was not back, and he had been removed from where he fell by some of the women. He was now in his own house.

He decided almost immediately that there was no time to be wasted. There was no longer any problem about provoking a fight with Camlak. The problem now was to enlist support in making a formal affair out of the fight. Matters were coming to a head. The Communion of Souls would be declared soon, and then the bickering would start. Yami's time was over and someone had to succeed him.

Porcel went out in search of support. He expected it to be easy to come by, but he was wrong. It did not take him long to find out who it was that had hit him over the head, and with what. His standing in the village had fallen catastrophically. It was hardly any fault of his own that he had been felled from behind with a cooking pot, but that was what had happened, and his public image was in ruins.

His temper, which had started out bad, got worse.

38.

Yami emerged from the long house to confront the assembled people of Stalhelm. He was dressed in his ceremonial robes, and he was already deep in the trance state. The Chief Elders lined up behind him. They, too, were in trance, but they would have no part to play in the Old Man's declarations. They were present purely and simply for show. It was Yami and Yami's soul that mattered.

Before the Old Man came out the crowd had been making a good deal of noise. Camlak had returned only minutes before, with the main party of the warriors and virtually all of the field-workers, the stone-workers and the gatherers. Talk was flying back and forth across this large group with great speed and verve. But Yami silenced them all with a gesture, while he took up his position squatting on the high throne-stone. There he waited, until his audience settled.

"The Communion of Souls is beginning," intoned Yami, in his Oracular voice. "We must make ready."

There was a long, pregnant pause. The audience waited for Yami to proceed to the important business. The Sun had to be chosen, and the Earth, and the Star King. And the testing had to be determined.

Yami let the silence drag on. This moment, in itself, was a kind of test. This was the moment when names formed on every tongue, when every mouth had to taste the name it held, and decide whether to swallow or to shout. This was the moment when ambitions had to be weighed carefully, and either discarded or committed to the test.

Finally, Yami spoke again.

"Who will name the Star King?" he asked.

This time, there was no pause. Porcel stood up from where he crouched beside the throne-stone, and said flatly, "I name Yami."

Yami, in trance, was not permitted to react. He was not present in his own person, but in the person of his Gray Soul, and in the person of the Old Man. If he accepted his own name, as he might well be bound to do, then he would wake from the trance state not as the leader of his people but as their victim.

Not one of the elders challenged Porcel's declaration. They, too, had come to a decision in this matter, and they agreed. But Camlak, for one, was determined that the matter should not rest there.

"I name Porcel," he said, without rising from where he crouched at the back of the crowd. Porcel did not bother to react. He knew, as did the elders, that Camlak's call could not be accepted. Yami was an ancient, at the end of his life. Porcel was a warrior. If anyone were to be named who had any real chance of being Star King instead of Yami, then it would be an elder, or perhaps a reader. Not a fighting man.

But there was no other name. It had already been settled between those who mattered that Yami's time was over. Even Yami would have accepted that. He loved life as well as anyone, but he knew as well as anyone the way in which life was lived—and from that there could be no freedom.

"Yami is named Star King," said the Oracle, speaking his own name without a trace of emotion. "Who will name the Sun?"

This time it was bent-legged Chemec who sprang to his feet beneath the high stone.

"I name Porcel," he called loudly. This time there was a reaction in the crowd. Some laughed, others made vague sounds of agreement.

The reader named Orgond then nominated Camlak, and this nomination too was greeted with mixed sounds of approval and derision.

There was a pause, while the people waited to discover whether anyone else wished to declare his ambition at this particular point in time. And a third name was offered, and then a fourth. It was an unusually high number. But neither Porcel nor Camlak could be said to meet with unilateral approval, and this would be the last chance for a good many men who were passing or just approaching their prime, and in whom spirits ran high.

The third name was Yewen, and the fourth Magant. Both these men were good fighting men, strong and intelligent, but neither of them would have seemed likely candidates. Their ambitions had been nurtured more or less in secret.

Yami rejected none of the four names. A slight stir ran through the crowd when this was realized. Usually, these matters were settled directly between the aspirants, but the Old Man could hardly order four men into a ring to fight it out. Three dead men was a high price to pay for a Communion of Souls, and the winner of such a complex contest would hardly be able to claim all the credit of victory.

"The names will be put to the test," said Yami, still intoning in a low, smooth voice. "They must face the harrowhound. The one who kills will rise as the Sun."

Camlak felt his heart sink inside his chest. He had known that the time was come to face the crucial test—he had expected to fight Porcel in the ring. This test, however, was an entirely different thing. He would be at a disadvantage in a duel, but that was nothing compared to the challenge of facing a harrowhound. And in this manner of contest, he would have to face it alone. He looked toward the base of the throne-stone, and he found Porcel's face amid the crowd. Porcel was looking back at him. Their eyes met and locked. Neither man knew what the other would do.

Somewhere in the crowd, Yewen withdrew his name. After a pause of half a minute or so, Magant also indicated that he was unwilling to accept the test. Porcel and Camlak both remained silent. If either one refused, then the other would pass the test by default, and would not have to go through with the challenge. Each man waited for the other to refuse, and when each man realized that the other would not they searched for the courage to accept.

Finally, Porcel said: "I will kill the harrowhound."

It was a bold enough step, but one taken in bitterness rather than in courage.

Camlak had no alternative but to declare that he also would attempt to kill the beast.

The ritual then passed on, but as Yami—supposedly entranced—said: "Who will name the Earth?" a faint trace of a smile lingered around his mouth. Camlak was not the only one who believed that the Old Man, condemned or not, had contrived to have the last laugh.

39.

All forms of social organization are inherently repressive.

In any society certain "natural" attributes of the human being (that is to say, attributes determined by genetic selection, defined over a matter of thousands or millions of years) must be set aside in favor of "unnatural" social demands (that is to say, demands which are historically recent and selected by nongenetic processes). In order that society should exist and develop according to the precepts of the individuals involved, a certain suppression of "human nature" is absolutely necessary.

As a result of this necessity, it is inevitable that the individual in society should be the focus of a conflict. His instinctive pattern of reactive behavior and his socially conditioned pattern of learned behavior are at odds. The resolution of this conflict may take several forms. If the repression of instinct is total, then perfect adjustment to society becomes a theoretical possibility. Total repression, however, is itself a state of personal maladjustment. Society may enforce conformity by increasing the pressure of repression, but if this process is successful then society becomes an assembly of neurotics. If, on the other hand, society tries to reorganize in order to allow instinctive patterns some limited contexts for expression, the entire social unit will become "neurotic" in that it will always exhibit self-threatening symptoms.

The Euchronian Movement wished to create a stable society. It needed such a high level of organization in order that the Plan could be completed that total repression and conformity seemed imperative. However, the ultimate aim of the Movement was to create a society where repression would be minimal. The Movement therefore faced a dilemma. In searching for a way to sidestep the whole problem, it came up with the i-minus effect.

The i-minus agent did not do away with instincts altogether, it merely prevented them from having any influence on behavior patterns.

Instincts are programmed into the genetic heritage of the individual. But the behavior patterns signified by the instincts still have to be learned. There has to be a process by which the purely physical language of the genes has to be translated into the conceptual language of the mind. An individual learns to behave instinctively in exactly the same way that he learns to behave socially—by repetition and rehearsal. The conscious mind provides one arena for such rehearsal, but *only* for consciously observed behavior—that is to say, social behavior. The conscious mind does not have direct access to the instincts.

There is, however, a second arena in which behavior may be rehearsed and learned, and that is the arena of dreams.

Animal dreams consist entirely of rehearsals of instinctive patterns of behavior. When an animal dreams its brain operates exactly as if the animal were awake and active, except that all motor stimuli to the body are short-circuited by a body known as the pons. If the pons is prevented from carrying out its function by surgery, animals can be observed "acting out" their dreams. Sleeping cats go through the motions of hunting, stalking, eating and the full range of sexual behavior. Everything which an animal does not learn from real experience it learns from "unreal" experience in its dreams.

In animals there is rarely any conflict between the behavior patterns learned from external experience and those learned from internal experience. Animals live the life which is laid down for them in their genetic heritage. They never try to be anything different. The only time that they are forced into conflict is when they are forced to be something other than they were "intended" to be by man. Only domestic animals and animals in zoos tend to become neurotic, and they tend to become neurotic because what they are taught by their manmade environment conflicts with what they are taught by their instincts.

In man himself, however, the situation is very much more complicated. Man *does* try, continually, to be something other than instinct would make him. This is the consequence of mental evolution to the point where the conscious mind obtains means of control and influence over the subconscious. Once a species evolves intelligence and self-consciousness, then its development races far ahead of the slow process of instinctive evolution. The trouble is that instincts can only be reshaped by natural selection—a tortuously slow process—while society can be remolded continuously by will power in the service of the active conscious mind. In the human being, the arena of dreams becomes an arena indeed—a battleground where learning and belief and imagination conflict terribly with the rehearsal of instinctive behavior patterns. In a human being, a dream is at best enigmatic and at worst maddening. All human beings are domestic animals or animals in a zoo—creatures in conflict—and the only answer provided by the power of the mind is repression, which is not a cure but merely an alleviation of the symptoms.

The i-minus agent devised by the Euchronian Movement during the years of the Plan changed all that. The i-minus agent was a selective genetic inhibitor which prevented all forms of genetic translation into the arena of dreams. The *only* input into the dreams of Euchronia's citizens was the input of real experience.

The theory was that this would lead to perfect social adjustment. The theory was only half-right. The citizens of Euchronia dreamed on, and their dreams were not devoid of conflict. But that conflict was muted very considerably indeed, and it was conflict of a rather different kind—a purely intellectual conflict of ideas and opinions.

The i-minus agent was administered in secret to the struggling millions who made themselves subject to the Euchronian Movement—in the food and in the water. In large measure, the i-minus project was responsible for the completeness of the dedication lent to the Plan by the people committed to it. One could not argue that the Plan would have been impossible without the i-minus agent, but it would certainly have taken much longer to complete.

When the Millennium was declared, the custodians of the

secret decided that the project should be maintained in the interests of promoting adjustment to the new social régime. They
formed a close council and laid down the rule that the council
should perpetuate itself by coopting new members to replace
those who died. The power of the close council in this matter
was to be administrative—other men who were party to the
secret (scientists, for the most part, and some civil servants in
charge of food production and mobilization) agreed to abide by
the majority decision of that council.

It was generally agreed that in order to remain effective the
i-minus effect had to be secret. Otherwise, any individual who
cared to do so might exempt himself.

The simple fact was, however, that the Euchronian Millennium
did not see any very rapid adjustment to the new social environment. Blocking the instinctive input into dreams was simply
not enough to guarantee Utopia—not, at any rate, in a matter
of decades. The intellectual conflict continued unchecked, and
the society of the Euchronian Millennium continued to reflect
that conflict.

On the other hand, had the i-minus project been abandoned,
Euchronian society might have been considerably worse off.
One does not eliminate conflict by introducing new conflicts.
The moral question of whether or not i-minus was justified was,
of course, a different one. Opinions varied greatly.

In the meantime, Euchronia's citizens had relatively peaceful
sleep, and nobody suffered from nightmares. Until Carl
Magner....

40.

Julea was sitting in the garden, supposedly reading, but not
really paying much attention to the book. The sun was high and
hot, and she had eaten a heavy meal. She might have drifted off
into sleep had it not been for the fact that she was saturated with
sleep. She slept long hours these days—as long as she could.

A man's shadow fell across her couch.

"Oh," she said, peering upwards, squinting against the light of the sun. "It's you."

Thorold Warnet sat down on the grass, and reached out a hand to toy with a rose which grew behind the couch.

"Has he come back?" he asked.

"No," she said. "Did you come through the house or climb over the wall?"

He shrugged. "I didn't want to disturb your father."

"He knows far more about all this than I do," she said.

"He doesn't know what I want to know."

"What makes you think I do?" she demanded. "All this is nothing to do with me. I don't have bad dreams, and I don't write books. I'm tired of the arguments. I don't really have an opinion, one way or the other, and I know that whatever anyone says the Underworld *isn't* going to be opened, so why don't you go argue with someone else?"

"I didn't come to argue," said Warnet. "I came to find out what Ryan knew that he told you, and that you told Joth. That's all."

"If you're sure that's what happened how is it that you don't know what it is that was passed so mysteriously along the chain of communication?"

"Because you haven't told me yet."

"I won't," she said. "Why should I? You're a Eupsychian."

"I'm not a criminal," he said. "Just a heretic. A Eupsychian is as entitled to be interested in the Underworld as anyone else. Both your brothers have gone down there. I know why Ryan went. He was properly equipped and others went with him. He knew what he was doing, to some extent. But Joth made no preparations, and he didn't tell anyone he was going—except you. He had no equipment, and no real reason. That seems odd to me, if not to anyone else. It suggests to me that perhaps Joth *didn't* intend to disappear. Perhaps he only wanted to look at the Underworld. Perhaps he only wanted to know how to get down. Perhaps something unexpected happened. Your father doesn't know. He doesn't know anything. I think you do."

"Why should I tell you, if I haven't even told my father?" she asked.

"Why shouldn't you tell me?" he countered. "*And* your father? Why keep it a secret?"

"Because Ryan told me not to tell anyone," she said quietly.

"But you did," Warnet said, also quietly. "You told Joth."

"Exactly," she said.

"Don't you want to know what happened to Joth?" he asked.

"Nothing's happened to Joth. I'm waiting for him to come back. That's all."

"He might not," said Warnet.

She wouldn't answer that comment. She pretended to look at her book.

"We can help you," persisted the Eupsychian. "We can find out what *did* happen, if you give us the chance. We can find the truth. Or is that what you're afraid of? Perhaps you'd rather *not* face the truth? Perhaps you'd rather pretend?"

"Perhaps," she said, coldly.

"Is your father's book a true account of life in the Underworld?" he asked.

"No," she said.

"But you don't know that. Nobody knows that except Ryan and his companions. And perhaps Joth. Possibly Joth."

"There's no point," she said, her voice breaking slightly into a tremulous whisper.

"Just *tell* me," he pleaded. "Just tell me what it is that led Joth to do whatever he did."

She hovered on the brink of tears. Rather than give way to them, she gave way to the questions.

"Ryan told me there was a man," she said. "A man who had been into the Underworld. Not just once. Lots of times. That's how Ryan knew how to get down into the Underworld. He said this man knew several routes, and used them. He thought it would be safe. But it wasn't. It couldn't have been. I didn't want to tell anybody." Ryan told me there was a man," she said. "A man who had been into the Underworld. Not just once. Lots of times. That's how Ryan knew how to get down into the Underworld. He said this man knew several routes, and used them. He thought it would be safe. But it wasn't. It couldn't have been. I didn't want to tell anybody."

"But you told Joth."

"Yes. And Joth's gone too. I shouldn't have let him go. Not after Ryan didn't come back. He went to find the man—went to find out about him. And he hasn't come back either."

"What's his name?" asked Warnet, softly.

"Jervis Burstone," she said.

41.

Carl Magner watched the young man disappear at the bottom of the garden. He was too far away to make out any details, and a little too distraught to care overmuch. Later, however, he went out to speak to his daughter about the visitor.

She explained what Warnet had wanted, but she lied, saying that she knew nothing and had told him nothing. There was nothing which could make her send her father after her two brothers. She hoped that Warnet would find out about Burstone and make sure that no one else ever went down into the world below.

"I was dreaming again," Magner told her. "The dream is always there. It's only a matter of time before it's there while I wake as well as while I sleep. The people...I see them all the more clearly every time...I only wish that someone could really understand."

"Yes," she said, inaudibly. "I wish that someone could."

42.

Joth woke screaming from his nightmare.

Huldi rolled over and put her hand over his mouth, pressing

hard to squeeze him into silence. When she was sure that he was finished she let her fingers go limp, and lifted them slowly.

Joth lay perfectly still, his spine rigid. He let out his tongue to lick the sweat from his upper lip. It tasted of Huldi's hand.

"It's going," he whispered, his tone undulating on the soft whistle of his fast-drawn breath. "It's going. Farther and farther."

"What?" she asked. "What was it?"

"I don't know," he said, fearfully. "I don't know. Already. It's going away. I can't remember. I didn't see. I don't know."

"It's only a dream," she said, putting her fingers back to his face. She touched his lips briefly, then let them linger on his cheek. His face was hot and dry. The only sweat was the sweat that came from her hand. He licked his own fingers and drew them across his forehead. There was water in a bowl not far away, but he could not reach it while his back was still rigid. Somehow, for some strange reason, he dared not move.

"It wasn't the same," he said. "It wasn't the same dream. Not at all. There was nothing...nothing at all...it was...insane. Crazy. I'm going mad."

"It was only a dream," whispered Huldi. "Only a dream."

"Not the same," he muttered.

Camlak drew aside the curtain and stood in the doorway, ring at them. The room behind him was lamplit, but the room which Joth and Huldi shared was pitch dark. Nevertheless, by some complex line of reflection, they could see a glint in Camlak's eyes.

Huldi flinched, fearing that they had disturbed him. But he spoke to them in a low voice, with no hint of anger.

"They came back a few minutes ago," he said. "The harrow-hound has killed Porcel. It is time for me to go."

43.

Camlak sniffed the air. He made a small sound in his throat, something between a cough and a purr. It was wordless and meaningless, an animal sound. For the time being, he was not wholly a man, because he had retreated into the cave of his mind, so that the Gray Soul could simulate something of the beast in him. Something of the harrowhound. A hunter needs to identify with his quarry. It is what makes him a hunter. Camlak made the animal sound for its own sake. It was not communicative.

The others were some way behind him. Chemec was there, and Magant and Cicon. The warriors of the village come to sit in lofty judgment over their kindred. A judgment from apart, without decision or participation. Only Porcel was not with them. Porcel was already dead.

If Camlak died too...well then, the bickering would begin all over again. They would cast dice for the pleasure of taking Yami's head. They would cast dice for Huldi, too, and Joth... they would let blood in full confidence because both Porcel and Camlak had spilled all theirs in the test. They would let blood in fear and in hope that they could continue to do so—in the war against Ermold's raiders.

Camlak carried a long knife and a short spear. The knife was beaten metal—soft, tainted Underworld metal which decayed and splintered, not the hard steel of the world above. The spear was tipped with bone—the bone of a harrowhound—and its shaft had been dressed in the blood of a harrowhound. A hunter must identify his weapons with his quarry.

In this fight there would be no help from Heaven at all. Camlak had nothing which was not his own. This was a man's challenge and there was more at stake than life and death.

There was a group of warriors peeling away from the main party, away to the left. Another would begin working its way to the right in a matter of moments. They carried drums and horns—their purpose was not to kill but to herd. They were to make sure that the harrowhound would not run. It was not the way of the harrowhound to avoid a challenge, but the beast had already fought once, and had eaten its fill of the victory. Camlak knew that he had an advantage over the beast which Porcel had not. But that was the luck of the draw. Nothing is decided by fitness alone. There is always the random factor. But the fact that he faced a slower, perhaps less ferocious, harrowhound did not make Camlak's test an easy one. It was still, perhaps, the ultimate test of all.

Camlak had to offer himself to the hunting-beast, to make it clear that they were fighting under rules. The harrowhound would understand. It would know that the fight was one-to-one and that if it won it would be allowed to run free. Until the hunters came again.

Not one of the warriors following Camlak had ever faced such an enemy alone, for all that they were men of courage and strength. In the normal course of events it would not occur to four or five hunters to track a harrowhound to the kill. Ten men might, but any less would content themselves with defending life and property. Even in a grand hunt, when twenty or thirty men might set out to corner and kill a hound, it was accepted that one man or two might die. Many such parties considered themselves fortunate to return home two men short, with only one huge head to show for it.

There could be no possible doubt that Porcel, given the choice, would far rather have faced a man than a harrowhound, even if he considered the advantage to be against him. But Camlak was not so sure. He was not, by nature, a fighting man. He had not the taste for man-killing. Hunting was entirely different, even hunting a man-beast. He would not have felt at ease facing Porcel in a ring. But in confrontation with a harrowhound, he *was* at ease. He had true confidence in the idea that this was *the* way of life. The killing of men—even Men Without Souls, to some extent—he thought of as Yami's way, which was an altogether different thing.

In a slender gully, where a stream ran slowly, and thin, dry spikestalks pushed their way up from cracks in bare rock, the harrowhound decided to make its stand. It knew what was happening because of the drums. It knew that it was called upon to kill or be killed. It knew enough to select its own ground. It was an intelligent beast, though its world was devoid of how and why and measured time. It was a thinking beast, a calculating beast. It knew the odds, and it knew the odds were in its favor. It waited in the gully, preparing itself for the contest, adjusting its state of mind. Its brown eyes gleamed with tear-reflected starlight. Its tongue lolled from its great mouth, stirring slightly and sliding back and forth across the crowns of its savage teeth.

It was not smiling.

Neither was Camlak, who came slowly up the gully, deliberately relaxing his muscles and his mind, tautening his spirit and trying to attract his Gray Soul out of the wilderness of nowhere and into the battle.

The drums slowed and stopped, and the last mournful notes of the horns died a lingering death. The warriors of the Children of the Voice aligned themselves along the gaping, twisted lips which ridged the gully, and they looked down from their vantage, eager to appreciate the coming conflict. The combatants seemed to be a long time coming to the climactic moment of their meeting. The harrowhound moved not at all, and Camlak seemed as though he were walking through water.

The great beast stood nearly as tall on four legs as Camlak stood on two. Only its head seemed out of proportion (too small) and even this impression was offset by its vast luminous brown eyes. Camlak wore a little armor, but it was only hide and bone—the natural armor of the harrowhound (thick, matted hair) was probably more efficient, and certainly more comfortable. Camlak also carried weapons, but these too seemed little enough compared to the natural weapons of the beast—the knives set in the hound's jaws were as sharp and strong as his, and *alive*. The massive callused paws were frightening clubs.

They faced each other, locked eyes, and showed themselves. Camlak did not stop his slow march forward. He was balanced lightly on his feet, his short tail held rigid, his own tiny jaws held slightly agape.

The beast looked at him somberly, fearlessly. It sensed, somehow, that even the assembled crowd was in the balance.

They were not committed to Camlak—they did not know whether or not they wanted him to win.

The harrowhound moved forward, closing the distance between itself and the oncoming hunter in a couple of long, loping strides. It expected the man to pause, or even to fall back, jockeying for position, trying to spy a mark for the spear, preparing a sequence of moves which might inflict a blow without taking one in return. But Camlak did not fall back and try to set himself up to receive the charge. On the crest of a sudden wave of terror, Camlak surged forward.

The harrowhound howled with terrifying volume as it launched itself from its back legs, already too close for the leap to be timed to perfection.

Camlak's soft hiss was lost in the howl, and to the watchers on the ridge it seemed that his body was lost too, disappeared into the belly of the hound as the hunter moved the wrong way.

The head of the beast came down, jaws reaching apart, the whiteness of teeth gleaming in the starlight.

The closeness of the bodies made it difficult to see what might be happening. The warriors expected that Camlak would have plunged his spear into the off-white underbelly of the beast, and thrust his knife up at the threatening head. They knew, as the beast must have known, that neither attack could do any lasting damage. The spear-point would stick in the muscle if it penetrated the hide. It could not get past the ribs to the pleural cavity. The thrust into the mouth might draw blood and cause pain, but the blade could not possibly reach a vital point *via* the skull. But the watchers could not see what Camlak did—they could only guess.

For a fleeting second Camlak believed that he was lost and dead, but he was not. Somehow he avoided the sweep of the massive jaws. He had not lost or broken his spear. He still held his knife. He swung away to one side, out from the shadow of the monster, slashing at it with a frantic sideways stab. The blow cut skin and seared tendon, and when Camlak was clear and the hound came down its leg buckled under its weight. As the combatants drew apart the beast seemed almost to limp.

The warriors fastened their stares on Camlak to see how he was hurt. But Camlak still moved easily—without speed, but without brokenness. Camlak surged into the shadow of the beast for a second time, and this time the beast had little enough grace in its leap. There had been no pause to draw breath, no hesitation of fatigue or fear. The harrowhound's head ducked once, twice, almost pecking at the hunter. Somehow, the teeth missed Camlak both times. The jaws could not close.

Camlak, right inside the beast's spring, thrust this left hand up to the fold of skin beneath the chin and wound his slender fingers into the hair with a single convulsive twist. He pivoted on his arm, keeping his head low, and simply pushed the jaws aside as they reached for him. His knife slashed furiously, and with the same short-armed backhanded stabbing motion he lacerated the flesh of the legs which buffeted him. The point of his spear had gone down into the groin of the animal and the shaft had broken. He had aimed for the muscle of the hind leg and missed.

The full weight of the beast came down on Camlak from directly above, and he was crushed onto the hard stone. But he did not relax his grip on the hair beneath the animal's neck, and his own head was still low, still protected by the arm from the dip and snap of the jaws.

Camlak had difficulty breathing, and the reek of the beast's fur filled his nostrils. The harrowhound was confused and in pain, but it would have made no difference if it had been able to clear its fugitive mind and formulate some kind of plan. It had no resources with which to do that but instinct, and its instinct was not adapted to the present situation.

As the harrowhound thrashed its legs, man and beast rolled. Camlak still slashed with his knife, not daring to make any more positive thrust in case the blade was lost like the spearhead. The beast's teeth finally made contact with the man's shoulder, but they could do no more than rake the flesh. Camlak sank his own teeth into the stripped flesh of the leg he had attacked with his knife. The taste was foul and there was enough hair left to fill his mouth like a gag, but he bit as deep as his jaws had strength.

The hound bayed again.

Camlak took advantage of the roll to get free of the monster before the full weight pinned him for a second time, and he scrambled sideways, regaining his feet on the bank of the stream. His mouth was dripping blood which was not his own. The beast tried to right itself in a single convulsive bound, but one foreleg at least was hurt badly, and it had to turn away and dance backwards or it would have staggered toward Camlak's eager knife. The beast sought the slanting stones at the back of the fault in order to launch itself again but Camlak, still impelled by persuasive terror, had not stood still for a moment. He had come forward while the beast went back, and it was the man who closed the gap between the two.

But this time the monster was not to be caught. Flailing its forepaws, it knocked the little man flying. Camlak was tumbled backwards from the flat stones into the stream. His fingers scraped the bottom as the water soaked into his clothing, and they came free of the surface with a handful of fluid mud and thin weed. As the harrowhound's jaws widened above him, Camlak threw the handful of sodden debris into the beast's face. Then he dropped flat, back into the water. The hound lurched over him, giving vent to a single titanic sneeze. But it had no sooner landed in the stream than it was turning, blinded and maddened.

Camlak grabbed the loose fold of skin and tangled fur yet again, and jammed the blade of his knife upward through the tightly pulled hide into the beast's throat. He pressed as hard as he possibly could, and then leapt backwards, leaving the knife buried. The harrowhound reared up on its hind legs and plunged wildly, missing him by a considerable margin. Camlak looked round for the shaft of his lost spear. He found it and went for it, and the weight of the beast came down on him as it bounded the same way. The collision was almost accidental, and the jaws closed on air, but Camlak felt his left arm break as he was hurled to the ground again.

Nevertheless, he was free and clear, and the beast was still half-blind. Its breathing was cut off and it was furious. It leaped again, and once more Camlak evaded the leap, and this time he had the shaft of the spear in hand. As the monster came at him again he dealt it a heavy blow on the skull, which seemed to have no effect at all. Once again, the hunter was knocked flying.

The hound blinked its eyes clear, but it was still leaping without pause, and it missed again. As it landed it was seared by pain from the wounds in its leg and in its groin, both of which it had aggravated considerably by its frantic movements. It staggered and fell forward, and as it sagged on to the rocks it turned the knife in its throat. Camlak hit it again and again with the stick, and though the blows did no damage at all, the beast gave way beneath them.

Camlak, exhausted though he was, found the strength and the presence of mind to hurl the stick away and pick up a size-able rock from the shallow bed of the stream. Though he had to pluck it out of the water one-handed he managed to raise it high above his head and then bring it down edge-first on to the back of the harrowhound's head.

The beast was already choking, and it was hammered to the ground by the blow.

Camlak followed, recovered the stone, and hurled it down again on the beast's head.

The harrowhound would not die, but it could not rise. It had to lie, twitching and uselessly snapping its jaws, while the new Old Man of Stalhelm smashed it slowly with the flat stone.

It still had not died when the warriors came into the gully to accept the verdict of the test. Camlak sagged into Cicon's arms, but after a few moments rest he was able to stand again and walk back to Stalhelm. Chemec the cripple was allowed to carry the harrowhound's head, after they had managed to cut it off with steel knives.

His arm was broken and his body was covered with bruises but Camlak was undoubtedly the leader of his people. The time had come for the Children of the Voice to learn Camlak's way.

44.

Enzo Ulicon made very little progress at all in finding out more about Magner's nightmares. As data accumulated, his early suspicions were confirmed, but he made no significant discoveries. The need for diplomacy in approaching medical sources, and the need to be evasive in pursuit of what he actually wanted to hear, slowed him down and made him tired.

He checked cases of dream disorders going back some centuries, but discovered that the number of cases where no clear pathological reason for the disorders had been traced were very few and in no way helpful. He could find no convincing evidence that anyone else was suffering, or had suffered, visions of Hell during their sleep.

His scientific advisers, familiar with both the theory and the practical application of the i-minus effect, offered him ideas, but nothing concrete. In the end, he had only logic and suspicion to guide him in reaching the most tentative of conclusions.

"There's no evidence to suggest that Magner is a genetic freak," he reported to Heres. "And in his waking life he appears to be quite ordinary—or did, until the dreams started to get the better of him. I think it's real, Rafael. We're not dealing with brain damage or with instinctive resurgence. This is something else. It's real, and it's meaningful, if only we can figure out what the meaning might be."

"You think that Magner's a telepath?" said Heres.

"I do."

"Can you prove it?"

"No. But something's getting into his head and we can't find any source for it inside him. It has to come from outside. The question is, where? And how, and what does it mean?"

"That's a lot of questions," said Heres. "How about some answers?"

"Guesses," said Ulicon. "It's all we have."

"Go on."

"All right. Number one. The source of the trouble is probably the pons. Magner awake doesn't suffer from visions—at least, he hasn't so far. Thus, the visions come to him via some process active during sleep. The pons is the body which decouples the motor responses from the dream-simulation. The pons *might* be the receiver in the telepathic link. What kind of radiation is involved we obviously have no idea. The cytoarchitecture of the pons might offer us some suggestions. That research will take years, though.

"Another guess. If we assume that the input into Magner's dreams *is* coming from outside then it seems like a good working assumption to say that it's coming from where Magner thinks it is—the Underworld. Someone—or something—down there is transmitting. New question: are they doing it deliberately? If so, is their message beamed specifically at Magner or is he the only man capable of picking it up? Personally, I find the idea of a deliberate transmission hard to swallow. I don't think that Magner's picking up messages at all. My guess is that it's some kind of leakage. He's getting vast assemblies of incoherent images which build in his mind to the visions he's written down in his book.

"The big hitch in all guesses is just this: what contribution is Magner making to the organization and interpretation of this input? How much of what Magner has written is raw input and how much is his personal reaction to it? We have no possible way of making a guess at this point. Not without another subject or another input. We have no basis at all for any sort of comparison."

"It's just not convincing," said Heres.

"I know," said Ulicon. "Don't you think I realize that? I wish it were convincing. I wish we had a few more puzzling facts to help make a pattern. I wish we had a few more definite data to help us rule out some of the possibilities. But we just don't have enough."

"So what do you think we should do?"

"Nothing. What can we do?"

"I agree," said Heres. "Nothing. But you know that some might not see it that way. The important thing is to avert any kind of a panic. We don't want to be rushed into action by something we can't understand, and which might turn out to be completely meaningless. Our top priority, as I see it, is to get on top of the whole thing so that we *can* do nothing. We have to squash the whole affair."

"Publicly, yes," said Ulicon. "But whatever we do in public we mustn't allow this thing to drop in private. We can do nothing as yet, but I'll bet my life on the fact that sooner or later this plot is going to thicken. Tomorrow or next year or Heaven knows when, there'll be another Magner, or another message, or another problem entirely. This thing is only just beginning, Rafe. You and I might not see the end, but we'll sure as hell see more than we've seen so far."

"But in the meantime," said Heres firmly, "we have to keep everything under control. We can't afford to let this thing blow up out of all proportion until we know more about it. Much more. We need something to divert attention from Magner. Either that or a way to silence him."

"That's up to you," said Ulicon. "But if I were you I wouldn't turn my back on the Underworld just at this moment. I'd worry. I *do* worry."

"I worry too," Heres assured him.

45.

Later in the day, Dascon contacted the Hegemon with news of Randal Harkanter's party, which was just about to leave for the Underworld. Heres hardly listened to what the other man said. Whatever Harkanter's small expedition discovered, it was hardly likely to add much to the solution of the problem, which, if Ulicon was even half-right, had moved into an entirely new dimension.

For the first time in his life, Heres felt the strange sensation that beneath his feet there was a gulf, and that if he did not tread lightly the floor might crumble beneath him and send him hurtling into the abyss,

Rypeck was frightened, and that was something Heres could ill afford, especially since it seemed there really might be something for Rypeck to be frightened *of.* If Rypeck took things into his own hands and talked about the i-minus effect it would be the end of his political career.

Heres knew that the interests of stability had to be placed first. The interests of the community—Euchronian interests. Fear of the Underworld simply must not be allowed to spread. There were factions which would undoubtedly benefit from such fear, and which might even try and foment anxiety. It was by no means a good thing that the expedition to the world below was in the hands of a man like Harkanter, who was something of a scaremonger even over and above his heretical leanings. And there was Emerich, too. Emerich *fed* on the ripples in the Euchronian pool—he was a glutton for strife and distrust. If only Emerich could be replaced by a man with a greater sense of responsibility...but it was in the very nature of the media that they existed to shock and excite and stimulate. Emerich's part in the drama of life was altogether too popular to be threatened. An Emerich would only be replaced by another Emerich. That was the way of life....

Heres worried, all right. But he would find an answer. Some kind of answer. There was always a way of sweeping the dust under the carpet.

Always.

46.

The outstanding thing about Camlak was his toughness. In Stalhelm he might find those superior in strength, in courage and in intelligence. But there was no one else with Camlak's refusal to bend and his capacity to withstand pressure of *every* kind. In a sense, he was like his father, but while Yami's toughness and inflexibility had thrived on a policy of destroying all conceivable threats, Camlak's rested on a carefulness of a rather different kind. Camlak was not a destroyer.

The key to Camlak's character was an unusual predilection for doubt. He withstood the pressure of education; he refused to accept common opinion and custom. He would not admit that precedent was adequate justification. Camlak *had* to be tough, to have survived with his doubt. Under normal circumstances a fighting man cannot afford doubt—in the struggle for existence certainty is usually a powerful survival factor. But doubt is the doorway to discovery and Camlak's discoveries, assisted by a certain serendipity, kept him ahead of the race. He survived. He was not well liked, because he was not well understood, but he commanded some sort of respect.

The Children of the Voice were not, by and large, a cogitative people. Evolution had given them intelligence, a high degree of sentience, and the capacity for conscious, rational thought which is the road to self-change. But the use to which the Children of the Voice had put these gifts tended to be rather narrow. In the early days of their "rise" as a species they had been overimitative of the True Men and in the latter days they were overdependent upon the beings which they called their Gray Souls.

However, talents evolved to fill one purpose inevitably spill over into other areas, and the intelligence of the Children of the Voice did begin to express itself in other ways than the simple business of keeping them alive in a difficult environment and a tachytelic evolutionary régime.

Camlak's predilection for doubt might be regarded as one of the painful steps in the evolution of a new perspective. It is one of the earliest steps, and in some ways it is one of the most difficult. A hundred doubters may die before one makes a beginning at the task of breaking down the barriers to doubt in his fellow men. Camlak was something of an enigma to his contemporaries, but the influence which he gained the power to exert when he became Old Man might have been crucial to their development as a community. Circumstance was eventually to rob him of that opportunity, but that does not detract from the fact that Camlak was a significant individual.

Yami was disappointed in Camlak. The elder man could have wished for a stronger, more successful son. Camlak did, it is true, win the right to adopt the Sun role in the Communion of Souls, and thus to replace his father as the man on the throne-stone, but Yami could still have wished for more fire and direct-ness in his successor's manner. Camlak was unusually fond of his father.

Camlak's influence on his daughter, Nita, was considerable. If Camlak was an evolutionary step, Nita was an evolutionary adventure. She already had something of a new perspective relative to the rest of her people. She had the advantage of being female, and therefore less liable to fall prey to the hostile environment. The evolution of mind works, by necessity, more through the female line of descent than the male.

Nita loved her father in a fashion that was almost Heavenly. As a race, the Children of the Voice was far too confined to the fragile present in the living of their lives to project their emotions far into the unreal future, or to dredge up emotional jetsam from the dead past. The Shaira loved, but not in the same sense that the people of the Overworld loved. Their love was more momentary, less coherent, and discontinuous. Nita was different, at least in the instance of her relationship with her father.

Camlak was a strange man. Perhaps something of a tragic figure. Perhaps even something of a hero.

47.

The Communion of Souls waited for Camlak.

The injuries he had sustained during the fight with the

harrowhound were not serious, but they were painful, and needed a little time. One of the readers set the broken arm and bound up his ribs. He had lost very little blood and he was not so weak that he had to take to his bed.

While he rested, Ayria attended to him, but he preferred the company of the aliens. A few whispers began to circulate concerning unnatural lust, but such rumors moved slowly and quietly. There were few enough who dared trespass on Camlak's good nature at the present time.

Camlak was vaguely interested by Huldi, but he was absolutely fascinated by Joth. Initially, it had seemed to him to be a good idea to help Joth in order that the Children of the Voice might one day make use of him. Stalhelm had never had any direct supply of Heaven-sent goods, and it seemed obvious to Camlak that it never would have if Yami's attitude to strangers had been allowed to rule forever. Many of the villagers were suspicious of the tools which came from the Overworld, and even more so of the books and the learning which could be taken from them. There was always a reservoir of opinion which held that such things ought not to be touched and that the Shaira should live entirely by their own efforts and their own ways. But the usefulness of the implements and the quality of the learning which could be obtained only from Overworld sources ensured that this opinion never came to dominate the intellectual climate. Even so, the art of reading was a minority pursuit, and many of those who were taught to read learned only to enhance their status, and not to make any use of that which was written in the books.

Camlak, as the son of an Old Man, had been forced to read at an early age, and had passed the point at which he still needed to be forced. He became an enthusiastic reader, and he absorbed what he read, although much of it he could not understand. While the elders regarded reading as something of a mystic art—the extraction of useful and/or meaningful details from a matrix which was largely cryptic and unfathomable—Camlak seemed to take it all more or less as it came. His attitude was one of pure inquiry, and he did not believe in the commonly held theory that books were constructed in order to conceal and protect knowledge by burying it in nonsense.

Joth confirmed Camlak's opinions about the books, and he was ready enough to take Joth's word, though many of the elders would have dismissed it out of hand. Among Huldi's people the printed word was regarded even more superstitiously than among Camlak's. The Men Without Souls had a separate sect of readers—and they most certainly did conceal and protect knowledge in order to maintain their monopoly in it. The readers of the True Men were fake magicians and false priests, and the fact that they were known by their more cynical brethren as charlatans did not alter the fact that they had possession and control of something real and valuable, and hence the power to maintain themselves as a mystic elite.

Joth wanted to inspect the books which were owned by the people of Stalhelm, but Camlak was reluctant. Eventually, Camlak brought him half a dozen, and let him touch them and inspect them. Joth found that they were real books, properly bound and printed on firm paper. He was more used to reading the disposable printouts from the cybernet. Bound books existed in the Overworld only as collector's items, prized as objects rather than as information. No one maintained a library for research purposes or for recreation—there was no need when any work was available on demand anywhere and at any time. Joth came to the conclusion that the books were prepared specifically for export to the Underworld, and again his mind struggled with the mystery of Burstone, failing to find an answer.

"What do the books tell you?" Joth asked Camlak. The question seemed particularly pertinent because the books he was permitted to examine seemed like a random selection from the cybernet's stores. They did not seem to have any relevance at all to the Underworld, nor any special significance of their own.

"A great deal," said Camlak. "I think there is always much to learn from the simplest book, although it is not easy to understand. When we find out how to make books like this ourselves, perhaps we will understand more clearly what is put into them. Our writings are very different, and the materials we have do not last, so that the readers must forever be copying and recopying. The books are products and pictures of another life, and it is a life very unlike our own. So much we cannot find because we do not know. But there is still much to be learned, if you are content to listen to the words and remember. I think there are books which are pictures of meaning rather than pictures of life."

"I don't know what you mean," said Joth.

"There are books which say what happens, and there are books which stay still, describing, thinking, looking. This is what the elders may think is put there only to clothe the truth and make it strange. I think it is truth itself, but truth of a different kind. It is a kind of teaching, because it is against the teaching we receive when we are shown how to read and what to read. There is more than one reality—this we know. There are two worlds, and perhaps more than two. But there is also more than one eye to look at reality, and the shape of a reality is in the eye as well as in the things the eye sees. This, it seems to me, is what is in the books. This is why it is so hard to see with the books, and so much easier to listen without understanding. If only we could see...."

"See what?" asked Joth.

"Your world. The sky. The people. The things. I would not want to live in your world, nor to stay for more than a moment. But I think I would like to see. A glimpse. I could understand so much more."

"Perhaps," said Joth. "But the sun would blind you. At night... perhaps I can show you the world, by night. If I can find a way home—a doorway to my world."

Camlak was silent for a while when Joth mentioned doorways. He knew of no way back for Joth, but he knew where to look for one.

Meanwhile, Joth wondered exactly how the Overworld *did* seem, in Camlak's imagination. Could Camlak tell the difference between fact and fantasy in the books? Could he tell the difference between representation and interpretation, between analogy and reality? Probably not. A glimpse of the world beneath the distant stars might Well cause Camlak to reorder his ideas completely. Even a glimpse of the stars themselves... the sight of infinity and space...the Face of Heaven.

But Joth knew, as did Camlak, that a glimpse was all that was possible. The Children of the Voice had their own world and their own life and their own reality, in which the stars were electric bulbs and the sky was a solid roof over their heads. To the people of the Underworld a different Heaven showed a very different face, but it was nonetheless the Face of Heaven. Joth knew that his father's crusade was meaningless and misled. One of the things which had come to worry him about the possibility of his return to the world above was the prospect of explaining to Carl Magner that his dreams had betrayed him.

48.

The man that Joth became when he awoke from his long illness into the real world of the realms of Tartarus was somewhat different from the Joth who had run away from Heaven in pursuit of his brother's memory.

The new Joth dreamed, of course, and his dreams were plagued by the awakened images of instinct which had broken free of the i-minus effect now that Joth ate different food and drank different water. But the renaissance of instinct had come too late into Joth's life to change him drastically. The nightmares hurt him, in his head, but they did little more than hurt. It was not the nightmares that turned him into a different man.

The new Joth had new and strange perspectives. He looked out into a different reality, and as time went by, he looked into that new reality with new eyes, because—as Camlak had said—reality is in the eye as much as the things it sees. Joth had lost time—or, rather, he had replaced one consciousness of time with another. The whole idea of *change* which he embraced was different. Days and nights had gone, and with them had gone the metrication of time. He could no longer count time, and because he could no longer count it he no longer saw it as a thing to be counted. His temporal sensitivity shrank as the past and future lost their outlines and closed in toward the infinitesimal moment of the present. Events no longer took "a long time" or "happened suddenly." Things took the time they took. Things happened at their own speed.

Joth began to assess the contents of his temporal environment in their own temporal terms, not by comparison to the movement of the sun in the sky or the cycling hands of a clock which symbolize that movement.

Joth, awakened into the Underworld, wanted to go home. He wanted to go home very badly—it was his first priority. But the *urgency* of returning to the Overworld drained away from him because it could not hold tight to its meaning. From the moment he became conscious of his new reality, Joth was going home. But at the same time he lived in Camlak's house and talked to the people who used it, and answered their questions, and he waited for Camlak to show him a way home. He was not in a hurry, because going home would take the time it took, and that was all there was to it.

Camlak questioned Joth on a wide variety of matters, most of which were fairly trivial. He asked about words, about meanings, and about a whole host of irrelevant facts. Many of his questions did not have answers, because the questions themselves were meaningless, but Joth did the best he could to help the Old Man of Stalhelm understand the alternative reality which existed on the far side of the sky-that-was-not.

Camlak learned a great deal—perhaps a great deal more than Joth thought he was teaching.

Huldi, meanwhile, had a very different interest in Joth. Because the Shaira tended to lump her and Joth into a single category, and because Joth himself obviously thought that she was more like him than were the Children of the Voice, Huldi too came to think that she and Joth were of like kind. When she had come to Stalhelm she had come simply to escape, with no plans, no ambitions, no idea what might eventually become of her, beyond a few simple notions which added up to little more than a determination to survive. But Joth offered a different range of possibilities. Joth was a straw to be clutched.

Huldi, of course, was not a reader, and had no concept at all of alternative realities. She was a creature of moderate intellectual powers trapped in a single frame of reference and caged by a fragile, unextended form of time. To her, Joth was a supernatural being, but a being with some affinities with herself. Like, and yet unlike. Huldi quickly came to love Joth, with a kind of love which was very unusual, if not unique.

Nita simply built the presence of Joth into the fabric of her growing up. He was present at a time when she was developing particularly quickly as a person, and her mind was alert, alive and adaptable. She was learning from books, from Camlak, and from her fellow-children. It was no strain to add Joth and Huldi to her sources of perspective. She loved to talk to the man with the metal face, and though most of the talk went by her like water in a fast stream, it had its effect on her, and in due course it would be revealed to her as something important in her life—something, perhaps, vital to the self she was to become.

Time—Tartaric time—bound together the people who shared Camlak's house. It added a new facet to their collective identity. It made them kindred of a strange kind.

49.

The people of Stalhelm were gathered before the long house (all but ten warriors, who kept watch in the hills) making a great half-circle whose center was the throne-stone.

Camlak knew that the festival of the Communion of Souls, on this particular occasion, would bring him pain. He expected pain in the confrontation with his Gray Soul, because he was

Old Man now, and the Gray Soul would be very much more a part of him henceforth. In addition, there would be pain in the ceremony—pain of a different kind but no easier to bear—because he was to be the Sun to Yami's Star King.

The drums were beating in a slow, steady rhythm. The drummers crouched in the shadow of the long house. The beat was muted, and when the horns blew, as they did in turn, they gave forth long, low notes like the distant crying of nightbirds.

The firelight was also muted. The flames burned red and low, and the moths which danced in the smoke seemed to have purple wings. They seemed to the villagers to represent the ghosts of shadowed souls.

The circle was silent, though there were a thousand people, and nearly half of them were children, or at least unmated. The people were working at the pulp which each had taken into his or her mouth. Periodically they would add new leaves to the masticated fiber, and suck out new supplies of the bitter juice. They did not move with the rhythm of the drums, but took that rhythm *into* themselves, and united it with the tempo of their heartbeat. Deliberately, they slowed their own metabolism. Their eyes remained open, but took on a hard glaze, and though they saw still, it was not wholly with their eyes that they watched.

The elders, now in the role of priests, stood in a line behind the arc of the crowd. Their arms were raised so that their loose robes hung apart from their bodies in great voluminous folds. No breeze stirred the trailing cloth. The elders, as priests, needed no leaves to grind between their jaws. They reached for the inner sight using no more than the power of their minds.

Into the space which was clear around the base of the throne-stone came the Star King. He was covered by a vast robe of black which swirled about him as he moved, and his head was enclosed by a gigantic mask, also painted jet black. Both the mask and the robe were sewn with tiny sequins which caught the light as he came close to the fire. As the folds of the cloak swayed and swung, the sequins flashed in turn, fugitive, evasive stars in a cloth of absolute darkness. Inside the Star King was Yami, but Yami transfigured. He was no longer Old Man, but merely an old man, and his body had completely lost its straightness. Yami staggered and shambled around the throne-stone, and the billows of the sky which draped his tired limbs flickered with uncertain strength.

The Star King moved, hopping and swaying, very slowly, consumed by the tempo of the drumbeat. Inside him, the pathetic figure of Yami could be seen now and again as the curve of a shoulder or the bulge of a hand.

Yami: a dancing corpse in a black shroud studded with little glass stars.

The Children of the Voice steadily extracted the juice from the leaves in their mouth, and reached for inner sight.

Up in the hills, the lookouts closed their ears to the hypnotic rhythm of the drums. They ran their tongues round in dry mouths, tasting the bitterness of the juice that was not there, feeling cold and alone despite the cloying warmness of the Underworld. Their heads ached.

In Camlak's house, behind the trailing edge of the crowd to one side of the long house, the Sun waited. His head was aching too, and he felt slightly sick. Camlak was inside a costume which was colored brightly gold and silver. The mask which he wore was pure white and polished. It crouched on his shoulders like a great white eagle.

Time passed him by, flowing like molasses.

Beside him, waiting with him, were Joth and Huldi. They could see from the window slits, over the heads of the squatting people, what was happening in the circlet of bare ground. They watched Yami's bobbing mask, like a big black fruit dancing on a wind-shaken branch.

But Joth and Huldi could only see with their eyes. They had no real conception of what was happening and what was about to happen, and it could not have been explained to them. Camlak was already apart from them in that he was descending into the depths of his mind, guided by the seeing that was not done with eyes alone. The aliens could not participate in the Communion, not even as observers.

The pace of the drums grew slower and slower, and the long crying of the horns began to blend with it into a lethargic undulation of muted sound. The notes were tortured and sonorous, dragged into seemingly infinite extension, and the hollow, indefinite roar of the drums was like the waves of a turbid sea.

In the Star King's dance, Yami found that his feet would no longer carry him forward. The dance went on, in bizarre slow motion, but now Yami merely writhed, and the sky which he wore was anchored to the spot.

There was still movement in the circle, but it was the movement of another costumed figure. All that Joth and Huldi could see through their slit windows was that the new dancer wore green, and that the mask which topped the robe—a grotesque, huge headpiece shaped like the cap of a mushroom—was striped gray and green. The stripes were curved and uneven, and flowed around and around the mask.

The dance was smooth and graceful, and the cloak hung so sheerly about the body that it was obviously a girl—a slender girl—inside it. The girl slowed in her movements as she came closer to the Star King. By the time that she touched him, she was almost still, and she sank slowly to the earth, so that the outsiders could no longer see her.

The mask that was the face of the Star King dipped, and he too went down, out of sight.

Slowly, Camlak began the long walk of the Sun. In his hands he carried an axe, bladed with stone from the quarry of Stalhelm, honed to a perfect curved edge.

50.

Yami was blind. Not only blind in his aged, whitening eyes (the mask, in any case, was eyeless) but blind in his inner vision. Yami was alone in that realm of Tartarus called the Underworld.

As he went down on top of the girl he reached for his Gray Soul. He reached as far as he could, driven by desperation. He prayed. But he remained alone. He remained trapped in the cage which had closed upon his mind. He was isolated from the Communion of Souls.

He screamed, and listened to his scream echoing in the chasms of his being, but there came no answer. There was no sound at all. He was soulless. Abandoned.

Yami could remember that in the past he had played the part of the Sun, and played it to perfection. He tried to imagine that around him now was the *persona* of the gaudy, garish yellow sun. But he was imprisoned by the sky, and even his imagination could not set him free. He could not make a Gray Soul out of his wishes. It was beyond his power.

He was old. He had no control over his arms and legs. He had even lost control of his thoughts.

Yami was on his hands and knees, his hands placed in the dirt on either side of the girl's waist, his knees on either side of her thighs. She was absolutely still beneath him, absolutely quiescent.

He was forgetting who he was.

The Star King leaned forward, until his belly came to touch her breasts. The Star King was not breathing, not even alive. In the vacuum of his mind there was total peace.

Inside the gray-green mask the girl was waiting. Her heart was slow and her breath very faint and easy. She was alive, but lost. Without the juice, she had found her Gray Soul. She was with it now, though perhaps she was only marginally aware. It would be as though she was on the borderline of sleep.

She waited.

The body of the Star King was rigid, like petrified wood.

There was balance.

And the axe came down in a long loose arc, striking Yami's head from his shoulders.

51.

The black mask rolled away like a big black ball, the loose earth sticking to it and blotting out the faintest of its stars. The head was still inside it. Blood—a torrent of it—*leapt* out to flood the stripes of the gray-green Earth-body and turn it deep red. The firelight was very close. The rushing stain turned black in the orange glow of the embers.

The Sun dragged the starlit Night from the clothes of the Earth, and thrust it aside. It slid away, rattling like charred paper crumpled in a fist. The Sun lowered his golden body, reaching to part the gray-green robes of the Earth, thrusting his light and his life into the parting.

The Sun made more life. More growth.

The Sun and the Earth were bound together, the Sun atop the Earth, their vast faces pressed to one another. The face of the Earth ran red with blood, and the polished white face of the Sun was stained, just a little. Smeared, as though by a careless hand. But it would not show until the Sun rose again.

Inside the Sun, Camlak was like ice. Physically cold, rigid.

He had achieved penetration—that was easy, because his penis was equipped with a bone—but as the Earth stirred against him with the oceanic swell of the drums he felt completely unmoved, as if nothing was happening, as if he were remote from himself. His penis felt hard and bone dry. Thin, and steely, like a knife from the upper world.

The Earth worked, and he moved on her, gently, in a rhythm which he only half felt, and hardly meant at all.

He was conscious that the Sun was acting out its role.

But he, inside the Sun, felt nothing like a fire, a source of energy, a bringer of life. He felt instead like a dead thing, trapped inside a womb.

He knew that his mask, on the outside, was white, and that his costume was brightly colored. But inside the Sun there was nothing but darkness. He was still seeing with his own eyes.

Seeing nothing.

His tongue was dry, his mouth gritty.

His spine was like a dry stick.

His ribs were running cold, like icicles.

His arm, splinted and set, was absolutely dead and without feeling. Likewise his heart, his belly and....

Seeing nothing.

And then the horns dragged him away from the unlit womb, dragged him down beneath the surface of an ocean of light. Hot, red-gold light. And through the flickering, radiant matrix the shadows moved.

Silver, called gray: the shadows.

A lighter gray than earth-gray. A softer gray. The gray, not of Earth at all, but of something and somewhere incalculably beyond Earth.

In an aureole of golden light, he came face to face with his Gray Soul.

52.

Everything was still.

So far as Joth and Huldi could see, there was absolutely nothing happening. The sound of the drums and the horns had died away.

No one in the entranced crowd moved a muscle. Even the small children were silent and still. The priests, with their arms still upraised, seemed as if they had been turned to stone.

Joth felt constrained not to move, and he dared not make the slightest sound. Huldi stirred restlessly, but even she felt the pressure of the occasion. Each of them was alone.

They had no way by which they could take themselves into the presence of their souls—if, in fact, they had souls at all.

53.

Camlak talked with his Gray Soul as an equal. He faced the being calmly, without the appearance of fear. He asked whether his way was not better than Yami's way, and the Gray Soul answered evasively. He asked many other questions, but he did not ask favors, nor did he ask advice. He spoke as a man might speak to another man (perhaps of a different race) and he listened as though he listened to the words of a man.

As well as words, they exchanged images, memories and emotional qualities. They conversed in many languages, of many different kinds, which contained many different varieties of meaning.

54.

The Sun fed the Earth with fuel, and life began within the Earth.

55.

Carl Magner was a self-haunted man. In a country of the bland he was a man with a very special sight. Not a king, but a victim.

In an age where a man born at his time might have expected to live a hundred and fifty years or more, he suffered sufficient psycho-physiological hardship to cut his expectancy of life to the ancient three score years and ten. Another man born the same day might have expected that his children would live to be two hundred. But Carl Magner had no such hopes of his own children.

Carl Magner was an emotionally isolated man, although it might be argued that the circumstances surrounding the death of his wife and the maiming of his younger son caused him to abandon the love of individuals in favor of a love for humanity in general which carried less immediate risk.

He was always a dedicated Euchronian, and became a fanatical Euchronian. Like any truly dedicated idealist he went far beyond the political boundaries of the doctrine and his beliefs lost their way in the wilderness of pure principle. The concept of Euchronianism which he eventually came to embrace was one which made many members of the Movement his enemy.

He honestly could not tell when his dreams began, or when the focus on a particular species of vision crowded out all other images. In the beginning, the dreams were only dreams, and were forgotten. The pattern, and the awareness of the pattern, took a considerable time to develop. It can be estimated that Carl Magner reached the point of obsession some five or six years before Ryan went into the Underworld in search of the truth. (It should be noted that Ryan's motives in venturing forth in search of that truth were founded on the hope that the truth would not resemble the dreams in any way, and that the obsessional hold of the dreams might be broken by virtue of that fact.) The dreams, as individual entities, probably began before the tragedies took place. Magner may well have been born with the seeds of conflict tainting his very earliest dreams.

Carl Magner was a big man, and a strong one, but over the years he lost the mental stature which went with his physique. He became increasingly brittle of temperament. One might almost say that in publishing *The Marriage of Heaven and Hell* he was preparing himself for another tragedy, making ready to meet it before its seeds were sown.

It was not Magner's wish that his son should go down into the Underworld, although at that particular time he did believe that it was important to verify the accuracy of his visions. When Ryan did not come back, Magner decided quite firmly that he would not be responsible for anyone's following in Ryan's footsteps. After all, by his visions, he *knew*. He was not the kind of man who would order another to descend into Hell. If anyone else was to go and discover the truth, it would have to be him, and before he went he had to deliver his message to the world.

His daughter might have told him about Burstone—about the fact that one man, at least, could confirm or deny his visions. But she did not, because she dared not. She was afraid of what might happen to him if he discovered that his visions were false. She was, perhaps, even more afraid of the opposite case.

After the publication of *The Marriage*, Magner was essentially a doomed man. The truth, whatever it might be, could only hurt him. He was a man at whom Fate had pointed the bone.

56.

Carl Magner faced the cameras uneasily. He should not have been nervous about his arguments, which he had gone over a hundred times before, nor should he have been nervous about exposure to an audience, which was what he had always intended. But he was definitely uneasy.

Clea Aron was wondering faintly what she was doing in the studio. She had not been interested in the Magner affair and she had no strong opinions about it. It seemed to her that Heres or Ulicon should have been anxious to take her place in the ultimate confrontation, but they had been quite definite in leaving it to her. She had a fairly dogmatic party line ready to deliver—something patched up by Javan Sobol and Luel Dascon, under advice from several interested parties—but she knew that she was not committed enough to attack Magner with any real vehemence.

Yvon Emerich knew that too, but he had no intention of letting his broadcast lack fire. In a sense, the choice of Clea Aron to represent the Movement was a shrewd political move, because Emerich would be forced on to her side in order to add bite to her arguments. He knew that, too, but it did not annoy him. He was content to be used by the Movement tonight, in the confident knowledge that he could balance the account another time. Magner meant nothing to Emerich, one way or the other—

if he was against the man it was only because the majority of the audience wanted to see him dissected. Emerich was only his usual clock-watching, super-organized self. It was all under his control: reason, sympathy, charity, morality. They were his to play with, because he was the eye of the people. And the mouth.

The cameras began to roll and Emerich introduced his "guests." He gave a rapid, inaccurate and rather insulting summary of *The Marriage of Heaven and Hell,* and then launched into Magner without further ado. As advised by Ballow he avoided the treacherous ground of how Magner came to write the book and whether the picture of life in the Underworld was factual or fanciful. He went straight to the moral meat of the argument.

"Supposing," said Emerich, "that there *are* people living in the old world, why should we let them into the new world which we have built?"

Magner, in closeup, seemed neither aggressive nor fanatical. His unease was under control. He simply said: "We have to recognize that there is only one world, and that we do not own it. We have no right to deny other men sunlight and clean air, and to force them to live in the excreta of our civilization."

"Isn't it true," said Emerich, hurrying along the obvious line which had been laid down for him, "that everyone in the ancient world had the option of remaking the world or dying with it? No man was forced to deny his children a share in the future of Euchronian man."

"That is what the Movement claims," said Magner, deliberately but indirectly challenging the truth of the statement, "but that was eleven thousand years ago. There is no justice in demanding that a man should bear the responsibility of his remote ancestors' decisions."

"So you believe," said Emerich, "that the descendants of the men who rejected the new world are just as entitled to enjoy the fruits of that new world as us, whose ancestors spent eleven thousand years in labor, hardship and deprivation."

"Of course," said Magner. "The eleven thousand years were years of Purgatory no less for their ancestors than for our own.

There was hardship and deprivation for everyone. It is not just that we should inherit Heaven while they are condemned to Hell."

"You are familiar, are you not," said Emerich, "with the fable of the ant and the grasshopper? While the ant labored the grasshopper was idle. And when winter came the grasshopper asked to be sheltered in the ant's nest. The ant refused, and the grasshopper died. Wasn't that justice? Isn't the message of the fable the principle that those who provide for themselves are favored over those who do not? Isn't that the justice of nature? Isn't it the way things are?"

"It is not the justice of nature," said Magner. "Only the law. We can make and change laws. We need not be bound by unjust laws. That is what it means to be human."

Emerich was ready and waiting for the answer. It was all as expected. He turned to Clea Aron.

"You are a member of the Hegemony of the Movement," he said. "You make and change the laws. What do you say to the argument?"

Clea cleared her throat, preparing herself for the first broadside. She was easy in her mind and comfortable at this stage.

"We are alive today," she said, "because of the efforts of the Euchronian Movement. If there are men alive today on the old surface, then they too owe their survival to the Euchronian Movement. At the end of the second dark age, the Earth was dying. The human race was foundering in the wreckage of the biosphere. It faced extinction. The Movement was the one force which offered a method and—more important—a motivation for building a new world from the ashes of the old. The Movement made a Plan—a magnificent plan—to build a new biosphere, a new civilization and a new society. The new world was to be a good world, and the new society was to be a sane and stable society which would never again allow extinction to threaten. The goal of the Movement was not simply survival, but *responsible* survival, in harmony with the new world which we were to recover from the old.

"We live today in that society. We have sanity, and stability, and comfort, and culture, and peace. Above all else, we have harmony with our new world. We are living up to the responsibility our ancestors accepted. The new world will not be destroyed by an age of psychosis. We will protect it from that possibility.

"The Euchronian Plan has passed the test—it has been fulfilled. We do not have Utopia, because we have not yet become Utopians. Perhaps we never will—that possibility we can accept, because we are human. But the fact that we may never have Utopia does not mean that we must sink to the level of our ancestors. We must accept the place in the scheme of things which we have strived long and hard to attain. We have a responsibility to ourselves, and to our ancestors—but most important of all, we have a responsibility to our unborn children—children born next year and *in the next eleven thousand years*. The one thing we must not do is abandon the responsibility we owe to our children because eleven thousand years ago the men who opposed Euchronia abandoned *theirs*.

"We tend to take for granted the countless generations of men who gave their lives so that we could enjoy a new world. The fact that we are here tonight is eloquent testimony to the extent to which we take it for granted. But we must not be allowed to forget that those generations of men worked for a *reason*—that they dedicated their lives to an ideal. They were building a world which they could not hope to see—for their remote descendants. The original Planners were not working for their children of eleven thousand years in the future, but for their children a hundred thousand years in the future. Thanks to the power and the determination of the Movement *we* have the world they wanted to build. We might just as easily be building it ourselves. And if we were building it ourselves, then I believe we would be content to do so. We would accept our responsibilities and we would accept them willingly.

The men who stayed on the ground were selfish men. They were interested only in their own lives, and in plundering what they could from a world which they knew to be dying by their parasitism. They acknowledged no responsibility toward their descendants. They did not believe that they would have descendants. We must remember that I am not talking about a single generation of men called upon to make a choice at a point in their lives. I am talking about a hundred generations of men who made their choice and stuck to it, and whose choice was reaffirmed by their children and their children's children. The men who stayed on the ground are an entirely different species. They are the children of greed and selfishness and destruction. If they live today then they live in exactly the way they have always lived—by plunder.

They have stripped the old world to its bones, and now they are fighting desperately to consume as large a share as possible of the wastes of ours.

"These are the children betrayed by their millions of ancestors. We are the children who were not betrayed, and who must not betray our own children. Our ancestors accepted responsibility for building a world, and we must accept the responsibility along with the world. It would be the most terrible of crimes to open our world to the forces of greed and destruction that destroyed the old."

Emerich knew that she had gone on too long, but he had allowed her to do so because she was obviously in good form. She had begun to repeat herself in the end, but she had rounded out her argument quickly enough. If she had run over her time she had only taken time he had already won from Magner. The stage was set now, the arguments were arrayed. The issues were assembled—sins of the fathers...Euchronian responsibilities and principles...justice and humanity....

All Emerich had to do was keep the wheel spinning.

"Clea," he said, as the camera hesitated between the combatants, "used the term 'betrayal.' Don't you think, Carl, that your plan to open the way between the worlds is such a betrayal? Isn't it a betrayal, not only of everything your ancestors worked for, but of your own world, your own life, your own children?"

Magner was tempted to say "no" and leave it at that. It was as simple as that, to him. But he knew that he could not afford it. He was backed up to the wall now, he had to hit back.

"Clea spoke of men betraying their children and men betraying their ancestors," he said. "I think that such arguments are themselves betrayals. They are traitors to reason and to humanity. Perhaps the men who did not choose to participate in the Euchronian Plan were selfish. But you cannot simply declare a man 'selfish' and write him out of the human race. There is more to a man than his lack of Euchronian belief. These men had a choice, and they took it, and we must recognize that it was not an easy choice, that their motives were probably complex, and that the fact they chose to stay with the old world rather than with the new does not make them villains, let alone subhumans of 'an entirely different species.'

"We must recognize that our knowledge of the early years of the Plan is imperfect, and that our understanding is even more imperfect. We live now in entirely different circumstances. We do not have the means by which we might judge these men, and it is wrong that we should attempt to do so. We have a new world now, and a new way of life. We have a responsibility to the men who worked to give us this new life—but we must not make this responsibility into idolatry. We have a responsibility to *use* the gifts which they have given us, to adapt our thinking to our new life. We are failing our ancestors if we accept our new world but stick with fanatical rigidity to old prejudices, and ways of thought developed in old contexts. We are new men now—the human race has made a second beginning. Then let us find a new and proper humanity—let us aspire to the justice that our ancestors lacked as well as to the sanity and the hope for the future which they possessed.

"I say that we have no right whatsoever to condemn the men of the Underworld for the decisions made by their forefathers. But even if we had, would it not be just and reasonable to refuse to exercise that right? In the new world today we do not hate the men of the Underworld. Why do we ignore them? Why have we forgotten their world and their very existence? Is this not an attitude of *guilt*? You want me to speak about betrayal...well, then, I offer you this betrayal: the betrayal of the men on the ground by the men in the sky. The betrayal of our kindred, of our own humanity. Do we owe our loyalty to a cruel principle, or do we owe it to *people*?"

"We owe our loyalty to one another," said Clea, without waiting for Emerich. "Not to a principle of any kind, nor to an idea which is, in the final analysis, only a label. You say that we owe our loyalty to people, but what is 'people'? Who are 'people'? We cannot define a man by calling him a man. We must have an idea of humanity which is not simply a matter of shape or the ability to cross-breed. You yourself have talked of things which are 'truly human.' We all have some idea of the qualities which go to make up what we call 'humanity.' We cannot determine our loyalties as simply as you seem to think. You say that we condemn the people of the Underworld—I say that they stand condemned, and not through any of *our* doing. We can owe them nothing that we do not owe in greater measure to ourselves, and to our ancestors and descendants as far as the imagination can stretch. We must make a decision as to whom we might mean when we speak of 'people.' And we must also decide what we include in our concept of humanity.

"I owe my loyalty to the men and women of the Euchronian Millennium—to the men and women who made it possible and to the men and women who will enjoy its fruits. I owe my loyalty to the whole human world fashioned by those same men and women and provided for them. I will do my utmost to protect that world from those who attack or oppose it—whether from without or from within. The fact that those assailants may be 'people' does not exempt them from all judgment of their actions. Sometimes, in matters of loyalty, one must choose *between* people. I have made my choice and I have made it rationally and justly. The new world must be protected by and on behalf of Euchronia's citizens. The men in the Underworld, whether it is Hell or Heaven, must stay there. It is their world, to use as they will."

"And the sunlight?" said Magner. "Is the sunlight ours and ours alone? Do we own the Face of Heaven itself?"

"We do," said Clea Aron. "We have built a world upon which the Face of Heaven may smile. It is ours. The men of the Underworld chose the Face of their own Heaven. They chose darkness. It is theirs."

Magner drew breath. The camera was on him. Emerich made no move to intervene.

"All that I say," said Magner, "is that they should have that choice. They should be able to choose darkness, if they so wish. But they should also be able to choose light. As you have said, it was not one generation of men who were offered a choice by the Planners, but many. I say that we should still offer that choice to the men on the ground. Now, and to all future generations."

"But isn't the choice you want to offer a different choice altogether?" This time it was Emerich who took up the point. "The choice which was offered by the Planners was the choice between building a world and parasitizing a world. No one offered them Heaven, but only the opportunity of working towards a Heaven for their children. You want to offer them the reward without the labor. That's not the same choice at all, is it?"

"It's the choice that *we* face," said Magner. "There are men in Heaven and men in Hell. *We* have the choice of delivering the men of the Underworld from their life of torment, or of condemning them to suffer it for eternity. They have no choice unless we choose to give it to them. It is true that their choice is not the choice that was offered to their ancestors, but neither is ours."

"In that case," Emerich pointed out, "you can hardly argue that we should give the men on the ground the choice because the Planners did."

Magner shrugged. "I accept that entirely. We shouldn't be arguing on the basis of what the Planners did or didn't do. But it was by reference to the Planners that Clea was trying to justify her entire argument. My argument is based on the fact that in the Underworld there are men like ourselves, and that we should share what we have with them."

"There may be men," said Clea, "but there are certainly no men like ourselves. I have already said that you cannot simply call the inhabitants of the old world 'men' and leave it at that. What *kind* of men are they that live in the ruins of a murdered world, subsisting on the waste of another? If men live like rats in a sewer, are they not more rats than men?"

"You have a somewhat prettified concept of humanity," snapped Magner, his voice sounding slightly unsteady for the first time. "If the new world fell apart tomorrow and pitched us all into this Hell the Euchronian Plan has created do you imagine that none of us could survive? Don't you think that we would willingly take to dirt and decay and waste and the bare bones of a ruined world, if that were the price of survival? Don't you think that in a matter of days the environment of the Underworld could have transformed you, or I, or Rafael Heres, or even Yvon Emerich into a scavenger, living like 'a rat in a sewer?' Man is an adaptable animal, Clea. What is necessary, he will do. Whatever is necessary."

"Perhaps," said Clea, whose voice accepted the edge of hostility and magnified it in turning it back on Magner. "No doubt *some* of us might do perfectly well as citizens of the Underworld. You see the capacity for degeneration in all of us, and perhaps it is there, in all of us, to some degree. All the more reason, I would think, that we should not take these monster-men into our world. If the seeds of degeneracy are in us all, then the third dark age is not so distant from us as we might think. We must guard against it all the more watchfully."

"You say that man is an adaptable animal," said Emerich, taking up the thread artfully and concentrating the assault on Magner, "and we must remember that the Underworld has been closed for a very long time. The men of the Underworld, there-fore, are presumably adapted to it. You call the Underworld Hell—but do they? Why is the Underworld a Hell if man is so adaptable? If the men of the Underworld have adapted to darkness, wouldn't it be cruelty to let the light shine into their dark world? Might not the sun be said to represent, from *their* viewpoint, the fires of Hell? In short, Carl, isn't it true that the men of the Underworld no more want a doorway into our world than we want a doorway into theirs?"

Emerich hammered out the questions in quick succession, with heavy emphasis on each one, and then just stopped, leaving Magner suspended in stiff silence. Magner, caught following the drift of Clea Aron's argument, was suddenly stranded by confrontation with Emerich's. The camera zoomed in on him and trapped him, caged his face in the well of sudden silence, closed in on his hesitation.

All of a sudden, his uneasiness flared into fear. His head, blown up to three times natural size, was cut off at the shoulders and held in a million holoviewers all over the world. He could feel the tightness of the frame, the claustrophobia.

"I said that man was adaptable," said Magner, arranging his thoughts while he spoke, and speaking slowly to steal time from the insistent cameras. "No doubt the men of the Underworld are adapted to their way of life. But they are adapted for survival. They survive, and of course they have adapted to the demands of survival under such circumstances.... But that does not make the Underworld any less of a Hell. There is nothing in the Underworld *except* survival. They have life, but nothing more. We have so much more, so much more to offer, if we only would. We can offer them the opportunities of happiness, of creativity, of self-fulfillment—everything that was given to us by the endeavors of others."

"We can offer these things," said Clea, levelly. "But they could not take them. They could not even *want* them."

Magner wanted to shout. He wanted to shout: "You cannot possibly know what they want." But that was the one thing he dared not say. It was the one thing he had to avoid at all costs. Because it was true. Clea could not know, and nor could Emerich. And all they had to say was "Nor can you." They had deliberately stayed clear of that point. They had waited for him, waited until he would have to stray on to it himself, or concede them the battle. There was no way out.

Emerich came smoothly into the gap, once the point was established as theirs.

"Isn't it true," said Emerich, "that we *can't* offer these things? We live as we do because we are a stable society. Our needs are supplied because they are carefully balanced to *match* the supply. How could we conceive of absorbing millions of people into Euchronian society? There is no way. The population of the world stands only in the hundreds of millions. Less than half a billion. How many men are there in the world below? Ten million? Fifty? We could not absorb even five million, could we? Wouldn't opening the Underworld *destroy* the society designed by the Euchronian Plan?"

Magner went down before the sudden torrent, which was not so much question as accusation. There was no answer he could find. A simple "no" could not stand up against the odds. It would not even be true.

"We have no right," said Magner, "to deny the people of the Underworld the sight of the Face of Heaven."

"We must," said Clea Aron.

"You say that they are the descendants of a selfish and greedy people," said Magner, trying to salvage something of the debate, though the moment was already past. "But we are a selfish and greedy people. We are a people who will not see, who are willfully blind to the world which still exists beneath our feet. We are the guilty, not they."

"Must we give away the world," asked Emerich, "because *you* feel guilty?"

"They survive down there without a world," said Magner. "They would not destroy ours."

"Neither should we," said Emerich.

To that, Magner could say nothing. He had virtually nothing left to say. He could go back to the beginning, and try to plot a better course for the whole argument, but there was not the time for that. They had trapped him. They had beaten him.

He had known, of course—since the very beginning—that the Overworld never would be opened, that they never would permit the men of the Underworld to accept a place in Heaven. He had tried to remind them that the wrecked world was still beneath their feet, that they could never leave it behind them, that it would always be with them, and that the people in torment would always return, one way or another, to haunt them.

But he was not sure that he had done even that.

57.

During the early years of the Euchronian Millennium there were six species extant in the Underworld which may be said to have been sentient and intelligent to some degree. Three of these races were descended from pre-Euchronian *Homo sapiens*, three were not. How many of these races might be called "human" is, however, a matter of definition. Also dependent on definition is the matter of *which* races might be called "human."

The so-called True Men (otherwise known as the "Men Without Souls") remained most similar to the parent stock, both genetically and culturally speaking. Physically, the True Men of the Underworld were not dissimilar to the men of the Overworld. It may be that interbreeding would still have been possible, and thus it could be argued that they remained the same species.

The True Men had, of course, abandoned all pretensions to the type of civilization characteristic of the age of psychosis. They had not begun to develop any kind of civilization based on an alternative pattern. They lived in walled towns, and though intercourse between towns was fairly well-developed there was virtually no political organization above that of the towns. The True Men were basically hunters and gatherers, with little agriculture or mining, but they retained the bare bones of a commercial system designed for a rather different way of life. The True Men tended to dominate those lands in which there existed substantial relics of the prehistoric second dark age, and the scavenging activities which they organized contrived to draw a certain amount of useful material from these areas even at this late date. This method of "production" served to keep the primitive activities of trade alive, but the source of supply was dwindling continuously.

The True Men retained literacy with the aid of material supplied by the Overworld, but the art fell under the complete control of a specialist sect, who thus became something of a power elite after the manner of priests or wizards.

Because of their relatively slow generation time the species was in slow decline under the prevailing environmental pressure. As a species, they were in no danger of extinction, but their way of life was being forced to undergo steady change, and ultimately they would have to look for an alternative.

A second species—or at least a subspecies—descended from prehistoric *Homo sapiens* was the Ahrima. Unlike the True Men the Ahrima had deliberately elected to remake their social organization and their way of life. The Ahrima may be regarded as an "artificial" species to some extent, because their genetic isolation from the True Men was a matter of rigid social ordinance. There is little doubt that fertile offspring would still have resulted from a cross, had such a cross been possible. However, the willful isolation of the Ahriman gene pool made it inevitable that they should diverge at a faster rate from the genetic heritage of the parent stock.

The Ahrima chose to become the predators *par excellence* of the Underworld. The founders of the species embraced a philosophy which declared that the only way to survive in such an ultimately rigorous environment was to give total loyalty to one well-defined group and none whatsoever to any other. The True Men and all other species of the Underworld thus became prey species for exploitation. The Ahrima were fighters, men and women alike, and they placed a very high priority on physical prowess, endurance, and the sheer power to survive. They did not practice specific rites of passage—such rituals were held to be false and ineffectual—but built into their whole way of life a rigor which ensured that the weak could not possibly survive. The total load on this species was socially increased, but it was also socially channeled to dispose of its random component. Owing to this socially promoted tachytely the Ahrima were slowly increasing fecundity and decreasing generation time. Simultaneously, however, they were putting such an intolerable pressure on the other major species of the Underworld that only two ultimate destinies were possible: either the remaining species would combine forces to obliterate the Ahrima entirely, or the Ahrima would wipe out their principal prey populations and have to reorder their own social organization.

The Ahrima fought without armor, unless one counts the masks which they wore. No doubt these masks did help to protect the head from injury, but their primary purpose was identification. The mask was the symbol of the Ahriman way of life, and no Ahriman would count a masked man his enemy, or a man without a mask as friend. The adoption of such an obvious and all-powerful symbol as the primary focus for social indoctrination led, eventually, to a strange form of pseudo-mimicry practiced by certain of the True Men. Occasionally, when a town of True Men was threatened by Ahrima they would put on masks of their own and join the marauders. In such an instance the Ahriman tribe would behave exactly as they would towards a second group of Ahrima which they encountered: the groups would move on together, and ultimately would fuse into one. *Ultimately,* however, could be quite a long time, and the simple fact is that the True Men were not equipped to cope with the Ahriman way of life. A whole town of True Men might join a band of Ahrima, and not one would survive the initial period of limited association. Undoubtedly, there was some introgression of genes from the True Men into the Ahriman species, but the process of selection involved in recruitment was such that the introgression was far from random. When a True Man donned the mask in order to save himself from death at the hands of the Ahrima he bought a stay of execution which would be served under difficult circumstances. His chance of getting away from the Ahrima at a later date was virtually nil. The Ahrima had a paramilitary organization and deserters were invariably killed.

The third species whose ancestors were prehistoric men were the Cuchumanates, whose divergence from the direct line was far more remarkable than that of the Ahrima. The Cuchumanates were almost certainly the product of genetic engineering, presumably deliberate and intraspecific. The Cuchumanates were parthenogenetic females, almost totally savage in their way of life, making no use of tools or artificial shelters. They moved in small groups or "families" (children were reared collectively) and were constantly migrating along established routes in order that their food supply should be allowed to regenerate constantly and maintain itself.

The Cuchumanates were not a warlike race, but would fight with great determination and courage if anyone attempted to displace them from their feeding grounds. As a species, they were in decline, but it seemed likely that they would survive for a long time as a rare and fugitive race. As conditions were perpetually changing it was not impossible that their ultimate fate might become more promising, but at the best their long-term chances of survival depended on factors outside their control.

The dominant species in the Underworld at the time the Euchronian Millennium was declared was the race which called itself "the Children of the Voice." Descended from prehistoric rats, the species may have been "aided" at some point in history by genetic engineering. In view of the fact that the species from which they evolved was the most highly developed semisentient of the old world, however, this conclusion must remain doubtful.

The Children of the Voice lived in walled villages rather similar to those of the True Men (probably imitative). However, while the village culture of the True Men appeared to be breaking up, that of the Children of the Voice was progressive and cohesive. Far more contact existed between villages, except when they were very isolated, and some semblance of national organization was in its infancy. The Children of the Voice were a quarrelsome race, but would work together consistently, if imperfectly. Their social organization was probably allowed to develop so quickly in spite of natural handicaps by virtue of the fact that their minds tended to dwell only briefly on emotional matters. Individual loves and hates were quickly forgotten, and behind those individual emotional reactions a more ordered conception of the world and its workings was allowed to develop. This manner of mental organization may have been correlated with the short generation time of the Children of the Voice, but undoubtedly their most important single difference from all other Earthly species was the symbiotic relationship which each individual had with a being he called his "Gray Soul."

The Children of the Voice regularly underwent certain forms of transcendental experience (drug-assisted, by sheer power of mind, or by pressure of extreme circumstance) which placed them in communication with these beings. Whether the Gray Souls existed in "another space" which merely came into contact with theirs, or whether the symbiotes were located wholly in the minds of the Children of the Voice themselves (but as totally independent entities) is not known.

The Children of the Voice were well able to sustain the load placed upon them by their environment, but perhaps less adapted to cope with the extraordinary pressures resulting from contact with other species. The fact that their culture evolved largely through "cultural contamination"—the imitation of the True Men and the inheritance of literacy and tool-using methods from the human-descended species in general—undoubtedly slowed their development as a unique species fulfilling its own needs and potentials.

Time, however, was on their side.

The so-called Hellkin were descended from prehistoric cats. They were a nomadic species with a high degree of sentience but rather limited intelligence. They lived in small groups and followed a nomadic way of life not too dissimilar to the Cuchumanates, except that they tended to be far more sociable.

The Hellkin were essentially peaceful, and maintained friendly relations with all species, except the Ahrima. The Hellkin were articulate, but had no real racial identity of their own, all their pretentions to culture having been derived by imitation of other species.

Their long-term future as a species was indeterminate. To a large extent they were culturally parasitic, but their parasitism was obviously facultative. They had untapped powers of survival. If the Ahrima were to become dominant in the Underworld the Hellkin might well become extinct or regress back to semisentience, but under all other circumstances they could probably be successful, integrating themselves into any social organization or primitive civilization without necessarily being absorbed by it.

The last of the six species which might be reckoned as intelligent at this particular time was the species descended from dogs—the harrowhounds.

At one time the harrowhounds were a successful predatory species. Like the Hellkin they ascended from semisentience to full sentience very quickly in the decay of civilization which took place in the second dark age. However, the harrowhounds found that their principal prey—the rats—were evolving faster and more effectively than themselves. By the time the Euchronian Millennium began the harrowhounds were nearing the bottom of a long and steady decline. Harrowhounds hunting in packs still showed a high degree of organization, and communicated very effectively despite the fact that they never adopted human language. But the solitary harrowhound was becoming ever more familiar. As a sentient species, the harrowhounds had no future, but regression might well permit them to discover a new line of development as a semisentient animal species. It is not impossible that their survival might have depended on their redomestication, perhaps by the Children of the Voice.

58.

Afterwards, there was a noticeable relaxation. There was no real end to the stillness, because the people on the ground did not return to their houses. But there was an end to the Communion of Souls, and the people of Stalhelm passed comfortably from trance into sleep. The priests knelt, and finally lay down. The crowd sagged and collapsed into a disordered heap. It was all over.

When the Sun withdrew from the Earth Camlak drifted into the realm of dreams. There was no real break in continuity between the vision that was real and the vision that was not, but he knew the difference, and he would know it again when he was awake.

Up in the hills, the lookouts also knew that it was finished. They, too, relaxed. They maintained their watch, and it was now easier for them to do so.

In Camlak's house, Joth and Huldi knew that it was finished. They had not spoken while the ritual was in progress, because they had both felt something of what it was about. But now they felt free.

"Your people," said Joth. "Do they...?"

"No," she said, quickly. Almost too quickly. He was not sure that she knew what he meant.

"Camlak killed his own father out there," said Joth. "His father is dead."

"He had to," said Huldi.

Joth shook his head. He did understand, but it was difficult for him to accept. "It's the way things are," he said. "But it's cruel. Your people—are they as cruel?"

She considered the question. It seemed to be meaningless, but she knew that he was looking for an answer. She decided, in the end, that the answer didn't much matter.

"No," she said. The trueness or falseness of the statement was irrelevant to her. She went away from the window, back into the room where she and Joth spent the greater part of their time. She had a sheet in the corner, beyond the crude bed where Joth slept.

Joth hadn't finished with questions and answers. He had read the symbolism of the ritual but he found it hard to believe. He could not see that it had any meaning for the people of this world. He could see no reason why the Children of the Voice acted out something which happened in another world—something meaningless to them. He knew that primitive peoples in distant prehistory practiced rites of similar nature, but they did so as magic. They did so in order to emphasize their identity with nature. This was not the purpose of the rite he had just witnessed. The identity assumed in the play was false—it was a pretense of an affinity with a world which had little in common with that of the Shaira.

Why? He wondered. What kind of magic was it? Was it magic at all?

"Huldi," he said, "what kind of gods do these people have?"

"They have no gods," she said.

"They have priests. They have religion."

"No gods," she said again. He knew that she would only repeat what she believed. She was incapable of discussion, of changing her mind. But did she know the truth? *Could* she know the truth?

"Do your people have gods?" he asked.

"No," she said.

"Do you have priests?"

"We need no priests. We have readers."

Joth saw, suddenly, that it might make a kind of sense. They needed no priests, the Men Without Souls. But that was not because they had no gods. It was because they had no rituals. The Children of the Voice did have rituals, and they had priests. But did they have gods? Did they *need* gods, any more than the Men Without Souls? Perhaps not.

What were gods for? he asked himself. They were the forces in action behind the visible forces of nature. They were the forces in control, the ultimate determinants of the way life should be—and had to be—lived.

The gods were the manifestations of another world, a world of which the experienced world was only a part, a world whose laws made sense of the wayward behavior of the experienced world. The gods were the determinants of the random and the inexplicable.

The Underworld needed no gods. The people of the Underworld did not need to imagine another world. They did not have to invent creative and determinant forces. Because there *was* another world. There *were* such forces. There was a world above them—a real, living world populated by men and not by gods. A world which, so far as the men of the Underworld were concerned, fulfilled all the functions of the supernatural world in a wholly natural fashion. The Overworld was Heaven, but it was not inhabited by gods. The peoples of the Underworld did not worship, nor did they offer sacrifices, nor did they beg for favors from chance. They had a much more stable and settled relationship with their other world than the primitives of prehistoric time.

The Children of the Voice were religious. They were not superstitious. The ritual which Joth had just seen was designed to fulfil their own purposes. It was an execution, and a communion. The symbols it used were the symbols of the other world— the *real* other world—and their symbolic function was wholly religious and not magical.

"You have no festivals," he said to Huldi. "No ceremonies."

"We dance," she said. "We like dancing."

"But you dance because you like it," he said. "Not because it brings the rain, or makes for better hunting, or for better crops. You don't dance to make you kill your enemies."

She didn't answer. She had no answer to offer.

Joth knew that the Children of the Voice did have beliefs, ideas which might be called superstitions. They did have customs which emphasized in various ways the identities of nature. Camlak had hunted the harrowhound with a spear whose head was made of the bone of a similar creature. But this was nothing more than an affinity with their world. They had no dominant, all-inclusive concept of the supernatural into which such small fragments of behavior could be collected.

No gods. No gods at all.

Joth realized then what the Face of Heaven really was, in the terms of the Underworld. He realized the mistake that his father had made in using the phrase in a context which made sense to him.

He realized that his father was very wrong. Even though the images were real, even though the picture was not wholly inaccurate. Carl Magner was utterly wrong.

Joth was still beside Huldi. He was kneeling. His brain was racing.

Huldi, already half asleep, pulled at his sleeve. The rotted material ripped, and he looked down, confused. Neither one of them was wholly conscious of what was happening.

Joth lay down beside the girl, and then he rolled on top of her. He felt the torrent of his thoughts begin to break up as he struggled with his clothing and reached into the folds of hers. By the time his head was clear he had no wish to recoil or reconsider.

He hesitated. But he knew what he was doing, and he carried on.

59.

Chemec was running down the slopes of Clauster Ridge as fast as his crippled leg would let him run. The other lookouts whose posts commanded a view of Livider Marches were also running. Signals were passed from man to man. One paused long enough to blow a long, loud blast on the horn which he carried.

They had been watching and waiting for the Men Without Souls.

But it was the Ahrima who were coming.

60.

Huldi was fast asleep, but Joth lay awake, thinking how easy it would be to escape. There was no guard at the skull-gate. He could draw the wooden bolts by himself and be away into the night. No one would know. No one would care.

He was indulging himself in a fantasy. He had no real plan to escape. The need which he felt to flee back to the Overworld was under control. He had faith, of a kind, that the need would be filled, in time.

In truth, the idea of going once again into the alien wilderness of the Underworld, away from the warm walls of Camlak's house, was a frightening one. He did not want to find himself adrift in that malicious landscape.

The sound of the horn captured his mind, and his idle thoughts died away. He was seized by a sudden fear, because he sensed that the crisis was suddenly close at hand.

61.

The foremost runner arrived back at the skull-gate, seized the stick from the wall, and began to beat the drum which hung beside the gate. His breath came in great ragged gouts and his limbs burned fiercely, but he swung the stick as hard and as fast as he could.

The village was roused within minutes. From the frozen sleep which the Communion had left in its wake sprang running men, shouting men, spreading the panic and the urgency like wildfire. Life was restored, and it found a furious tempo within seconds.

Camlak threw off the bloodstained mask and heard the cry of "Ah...rima!" almost instantly. He was still in the gold and silver costume of the ritual when the runner was brought to him.

"How many?" he asked, and "How soon?"

"A horde," said the runner, squeezing his words into the

breaths that he drew. "Crossing Cudal Canal. Too many, too close."

"Walgo?" he asked.

"It has not burned. Ermold must have taken the mask."

Camlak cursed. That would be Ermold's way. Ermold should have been born to the mask. There was no way that Stalhelm could survive. With the fighting strength of Walgo added to the Ahriman horde, however briefly, the masked marauders would smash Stalhelm in a matter of hours. The women and the children would have to be sent to Lehr, to make the best of their way to safety while the warriors tried to hold the town. The elders, the readers, the old women...all these would have to stay too, to bear arms, if they could...to take the place of the dead as they fell from the wall.

Death was coming. Death for all, unless Shairn could be awakened to the danger. Runners had to be sent to Lehr, to Opilion, to Digen. Perhaps the warriors would come out of the Heartland, to meet those of his people who could flee farthest. Perhaps not.

Camlak did not need to gather and command the people. They knew what the coming of the Ahrima meant. They knew what had to be done. Camlak ran back to his house, and while he discarded the ceremonial robes for armor he talked to Joth.

"You must go," he said, "and go quickly. To the metal wall in the north. If there is a way home for you, you will find it there. Do not come back here. If you come back to this world at all, go west, into Shairn. Ask for me in the northern towns, or make your way south to Lehr. If you do not hear from me in Lehr you will know that I am dead. Take Nita—she knows the map that hangs in the long house and she will show you the way. Take the other too—Ermold has taken the mask and she cannot stay here. The women would kill her."

There was no time to say anything more. There was no time to talk about the future, no time for good wishes. There was no time at all. Shairn was invaded and Stalhelm was under the spearhead of the invasion.

"Good-bye," said Joth, when he was ready. But Camlak did not even hear him.

62.

Simkin Cinner was not an important man by anyone's standards. The actions which he performed were on the whole quite irrelevant to the main current of life in the Overworld. But he was an *individual*, and not a representative of a particular type, and as an individual he had his own unique role to play in the scheme of things. He was a killer.

Despite the fact that he was a passionately patriotic Euchronian and fanatically loyal to the people of Euchronia's Millennium, Simkin Cinner was not a nice man. He was neither stupid nor ignorant, but ideas tended to come into his head from all kinds of peculiar angles, there to be associated into a loose webwork of opinions and motives which had no real relevance to his fanatical faith although they enjoyed its full motive power. He was self-deluded, it is true, but not because he was an idiot. Merely because he was superficial.

Cinner lived half in and half out of Millennial society. He spent a great deal of his time in the so-called Sanctuaries—the areas specifically designated as outside the organized society of the Overworld. The purpose of the Sanctuaries was to allow any citizen the ultimate freedom to opt right out. They also existed in order to give the Euchronians somewhere to put their criminals. The Sanctuaries were supplied, to some extent, with the raw materials of life by Euchronian Society—a gesture of goodwill and humanity.

Cinner, of course, had no need of Sanctuary as a retreat from society or a refuge from it, and he was not a criminal. He went into Sanctuary in order that he might appreciate Euchronia even more. He also went in to kill people. (Sometimes, it was expedient to have people removed altogether from the possibility of contact with society. Crime, in theory, was not punished, save by expulsion from society, but occasionally it was deemed convenient to follow up on that sentence. There were, of course, no laws applicable to Sanctuary. Freedom was freedom. Freedom to kill, freedom to be exterminated.)

Cinner liked violence, for its own sake, but he would never have dreamed of using violence against the Euchronian civilization. On the other hand, he hated to see the Euchronian civilization insulted or threatened in any way. That made him feel very bad. Full of violent feelings.

Usually someone told Cinner whom to kill. They gave him no direct orders, nor did they have to bribe him. It was sufficient just to indicate that it would be desirable if certain persons did not have the opportunity to "break out" of Sanctuary. The suggestions always came from people he admired and trusted.

Eventually, however, it was inevitable that Cinner would make a judgment of his own, and would discover his own reasons why a certain person should be removed from a society whose bountiful generosity he patently did not deserve. And it was inevitable, also, that the boundaries of Sanctuary would come to mean less to Cinner as time went by. Sanctuary, after all, is only a state of mind....

63.

Abram Ravelvent drove along the westbound highway. It was night, and there were very few cars on the road. He could make a good one-seventy in perfect comfort and safety.

"It isn't far," he said to his passengers (without taking his eyes off the road). "At this rate we'll be there in a matter of minutes. There's definitely a way down. One of a good many, I should think. I found it for Harkanter and his people, but I don't think they're going down until after the weekend. They're still getting together. I'm not actually sure what the thing is *for*, but the platform wasn't built in a day, and it wasn't turned into the Garden of Eden in a day either. There must have been quite adequate provision made for the transport of material from the lower world on a grand scale. I think this is only a door. There are probably much more impressive outlets. Many of the machines are built from the ground up, of course, and we still take quite a lot from the surface—or below the surface, I suppose, would probably be more exact."

Carl Magner made no reply. He was in the back seat, leaning back into the soft plastic, staring out through the window into the night, watching the blazing lights which whipped past the car so swiftly that their light became a continuous streak in the sky. He was hardly listening to Ravelvent. Ravelvent was no longer important.

He was going down into the Underworld.

Why? he wondered. Do I even know why? Is there a real reason? Is there any real purpose to be served?

He had no idea what he was going to do when he got down to the door which separated the worlds. Unlock it, if he could. Throw it wide open. And then? And...then?

Magner knew that the descent into the Underworld had become something of a meaningless ritual. He wanted to know the truth, but he knew—in his heart—that it wasn't the truth which mattered. Not to him. Ravelvent cared about the truth, and to Ravelvent the truth was important. But Ravelvent wouldn't go down into the Underworld. He couldn't. He was a coward, and he just couldn't face the idea. Ravelvent was scared of the Underworld and what it might contain. Perhaps that was why the truth was important...to him.

What can a look into the Underworld tell me? Magner asked himself. I have seen the Underworld a thousand times, I know it intimately—far more intimately than any glimpse from a tiny door in the wall of a machine complex. I know its life and its ways. I know it all. So why the door? Why, all of a sudden, do I have to go in search of the door? Never before, never in all the years...not even when Ryan didn't come back....

I can only lose, Magner told himself. I can only prove myself a liar. But can even that be said to be meaningful? What *does* it mean if I am wrong? Is there any meaning in it anymore? Haven't Yvon Emerich and Clea Aron and all their hungry audience proved my dreams, my hopes, my fears and my determination to be empty? All empty? Is there anything between the world above and the world below except a wall of ignorance and blindness? Can there ever be anything else? The Overworld exists because it rises above the dirt and the decay of the Underworld. The Underworld exists because the Overworld is above it. Is there anything more?

He could see some stars out of the car window, very faint because of the glare of the lights alongside the road. They were faint, silver points of light. They gave the impression of vast distance. Through the windows of the car, a glimpse of infinity. Beneath the spinning wheels, beneath the thin veneer that was a road and a world, a vision of Hell. In between, Magner. Alone.

For a moment, Carl Magner wondered what he had been doing, for the past weeks and months and years. But when he shut his eyes, he knew. The very threat of sleep was enough. He had thought his dreams a revelation. He had thought himself... he had to admit it now...privileged, granted a mission. He had seen himself as a kind of Messiah. Perhaps even more than that...perhaps a God. Hadn't his own sons, Ryan and Joth, gone into the Underworld in answer to *his* call? Christs, both of them. He had fallen prey to all kinds of vanity when he woke from his dreams. All kinds of blasphemy. He knew that now. He could see that clearly.

His dreams...even if they were true...*especially* if they were true...had been a kind of temptation, a temptation with a curse, a curse that had carried him to defeat, humiliation, and now to... what?

"You know," said Ravelvent, breaking up the silence with determined verbosity, "it's very strange. There must be so many ways into the Underworld. All I had to do was look, and they were there. So many. And yet no man of the Underworld has ever ventured up to the world above. Now why would that be? Why has there been no voyage of discovery? Why no invasion?

Why no theft? Why have they never come to look at the sun which we took away from them?"

Magner had no answers. It was Julea who spoke.

"It isn't strange," she said. "They wouldn't touch the machines. They wouldn't trust them. They wouldn't come near them."

"That's possible," said Ravelvent. "There are so many possibilities, with so many different implications. You know...."

He carried on talking. He felt obliged to talk, to mask his own confusion and faint trepidation. He felt that there might be some sort of pressure on him—the pressure of conscience—to go down the staircase with Magner. He knew that he wasn't going to do that. He felt slight guilt about it. He knew that Julea wouldn't go down—wouldn't even think of going down—and that he wouldn't be left alone no matter what. But he could envisage the long wait, the hours ticking by, the matter of deciding. Magner wouldn't come back. He was sure of that much. So what could he do? How long should he wait with Julea? Would Julea think that he ought to go down after her father, to search for him?

Julea didn't listen to him. She didn't need to. She knew that Ravelvent wasn't saying anything she wanted to hear.

She still hadn't told anyone except the Eupsychian about the name Ryan had given into her safekeeping, and which she had given to Joth. She didn't know whether this was right. It was obviously a secret, because *nobody* knew it. But whose secret? And why? And what did it mean? It was a deadly secret. It had killed Ryan, and Joth, and perhaps it would kill Warnet. One by one, it was subtracting everyone she knew from the fabric of her life. Her father was about to subtract himself. Who was left? What was the remainder? What was the answer?

All minus. All dead.

Ravelvent had called their destination a plexus. A nerve center. A vast lattice of nervous metal fiber. A reservoir of functional control for the cybernet. Gleaming threads of neuronal wire. Cytoarchitecture in pressed steel. Synapses in etched microcircuits. Metal-veined glass. Mile on mile of coiled plastic. A tangled knot of metal microorganism. A tiny fraction of the living leviathan corpse that was the cybernet: the Atlas which held the Overworld on its shoulders.

Ravelvent would send her father down into that. As if he were a bacterium oozing deep into the carcase of a sick body. Down and down and down, into the metal mental wilderness, into the deepest recesses of the Overworld's subconsciousness: Euchronia's id.

She alone understood (and only vaguely, in an instant of vision) the Odyssey which her father was about to undertake. She alone could see *where* he was going. Ravelvent and Magner were both sidetracked into *why.*

"I find it so difficult to understand," Ravelvent was saying, "why the failure to come to terms with a world which is only just below one's feet and is so *total.* I'm a loyal and convinced Euchronian, you know that. I don't believe for a minute that a society like ours is sterile. It's free, it's full of life. It's active, it's progressive. We haven't lost the dynamism of the Euchronian Plan, not by any means.

"But I could almost believe that there's some kind of *narcotic* aspect to the way we live. I could almost believe that there's something forcing our eyes away from certain directions. I believe, of course, that we must all look to the *future*, but I think there's a danger of becoming slightly obsessive, that we may become blind, in some way, to our present and the true extent that it has. I mean, when all said and done, we can't actually get *away* from the Underworld...."

He paused for a breath, waited for an echo of approval, a suggestion of an answer, a murmur of life.

There was utter silence.

64.

Cinner followed Ravelvent's car quite openly. He was not afraid that the other driver might realize he was being followed. Nobody would. There was no need to conceal a car on a road.

Ravelvent would not even notice that there was another car behind him, and that it was always the same car at the same distance. Suspicious minds were extinct in the Overworld.

The blood was warm—an alcoholic warmness—as it drained through Cinner's heart. He felt warm throughout. His heart did not pound. He was not excited, not jittery. Just pleasantly anticipating. He was perfectly assured. He was balancing himself delicately.

65.

Ravelvent pulled his car to a stop, and hesitated. His heart was thumping hard, there was a tightness in his throat. He opened the door, suddenly feeling constrained, and breathed in the cool night air.

The plexus was set back from the road, nestling between two shallow slopes. It looked very clean.

Julea got out of the near side rear door. Magner came out after her rather than getting out his own side. There was another car coming.

Ravelvent saw the other car when he turned to speak to his friends. Carl Magner and Julea were side by side, Julea was shutting the car door. He could see the other vehicle between their shoulders. It was dawdling, still slowing down. Ravelvent thought that it was going to stop.

For a moment Ravelvent wondered how he was going to explain what it was that the three of them were doing out here. What am I going to say? he asked himself.

Then Cinner leaned out of the window of the passing car, straightened his arm and shot Carl Magner in the back.

66.

The trek through the wilderness seemed endless, but Nita would not let them rest.

There was no road, no suggestion of a trail. They had cleared the cultivated fields in less than a mile, and once past the land which was under human governance they were in country which was totally wild. They had to fight their way through knee-high vegetation, wade through stagnant swamp, and scramble up, down and across rocky slopes.

Always the stars shone upon their efforts with absolute steadiness.

Their way was made easier by the fact that they had nothing to carry. Joth and Huldi possessed nothing save for the ragged clothes in which they stood, and Nita had brought nothing with her except a small all-purpose knife. She knew well enough how to live off the land. She had not even burdened herself with the map from the long house. That was committed to her memory.

Nita moved faster than either of her charges, and seemed never to tire. Huldi, of course, proved much more enduring than Joth. Thus it was Joth who determined the pace. It was for his benefit that they rested periodically.

"What will happen at the village?" asked Joth, while they rested.

"Most of the men will be killed," said Nita. "They will not keep off the Ahrima for long. A few will run away. The Ahrima will burn the houses, but they will not stay. They will be angry because the women and children have all gone. The Ahrima prefer to take slaves if they stay for a time in any one place. They will take what they can from Stalhelm, and then go. The work will be all undone, but it can be done again. When the Ahrima are gone, people will begin to come back. The land will still be there."

"What will the Ahrima do?" said Joth.

"Attack. Perhaps Lehr, perhaps Opilion. The Shaira cannot run away from every town. Somewhere they will have to stand. The Ahrima might run through Shairn without taking a town and slaves, but it is more likely that they will capture some good land, use slaves to strip it, and stay until the Shaira have mustered an army large enough to force them out. Then they might run, or they might try to get behind the army, to prey upon the villages whose warriors have been taken away."

"Either way," said Joth, "the country will be desolated. Destroyed."

The girl shrugged. "Hurt. No more. Shairn cannot be destroyed. It will always be here."

"Will the women and children reach Lehr?" asked Joth.

Nita shrugged again, apparently caring little either way. "If the fight is long enough, and the road is short enough. If the warriors of Lehr come out to cover their flight. Perhaps. Perhaps not. If the Ahrima catch them they will scatter in Dossal Bog. Many will be killed. Some will not. There are always some who live, some who return. The Ahrima will not be in Shairn forever."

"The men who took the mask will die," said Huldi. "All of them. In time."

"Even Ermold?" asked Nita.

"Even Ermold," said Huldi. Her voice was flat and self-assured, but Joth could not tell whether she believed it or whether she only wanted to believe it.

"Ermold could have fought the Ahrima," said Joth. "The men of Walgo could have warned the Shaira that the horde was on its way. An army might have come to Stalhelm."

"Then the Ahrima would have turned back," said Nita. "They would have taken Walgo, and all its people for slaves."

"The women and children could have come to Stalhelm, as yours went to Lehr."

Nita shook her head.

"They would not," said Huldi.

They went on through the empty, derelict world. They ate insects and drank water which tasted filthy. Joth made no complaints, and did as the others did. He no longer payed much attention to what he would once have considered rank foulness of smell and taste, but even so the sickness which had plagued him for a long time in Camlak's house returned to him, in some measure, in the wilderness. Often, he had to force himself on against the pain and the fever. But it was a battle he was winning, by degrees.

Joth had lost all notion of time. He had ceased to pay attention to time while he was in the Underworld, and was beginning to acquire the attitude of the people. The three slept when they felt sleep was necessary, and when Nita would permit it.

For a time they encountered few animals which seemed dangerous. They were menaced by no large predators, and they avoided snakebite and serious parasitism. They were slightly lucky, even in the early stages. But as time and the miles went by, all but unheeded, they penetrated deeper into the heart of the Swithering Waste, and they moved into a world as hostile and deadly as any of the Realms of Tartarus.

They passed through forests of shiny fungus as hard as wood—mycelia which mimicked trees, fruiting bodies like bushes. The ground was always ridged and slick because the bloated rhizoids and subterranean hyphae lay just beneath the humus. In every crevice there were clusters of small basidiomycetes, usually brightly colored and—so Nita said—poisonous. This multitude of tiny plants filled the air with an inconstant miasma of sporedust, and they all three had to protect their breathing apparatus with masks of cloth. The masks were crude and could not exclude the dust wholly, and all three found their bronchial tubes perpetually choking with phlegm. All three— but particularly Joth—suffered more or less constantly from allergic reactions in their sinuses and other mucous membranes. Nita made them take large doses of an extremely bitter membraneous algoid, which had some antihistamine properties, but it served only to ameliorate the symptoms, not to prevent them.

The ground was often covered with cockroaches and small black beetles. The dendrites provided a perfect home for a vast host of starlings and other, unknown species of birds which were hardly ever seen in the human lands of the Underworld.

In between the forests were wet regions, where the ground was either sodden or completely submerged. Here there was a different kind of vegetation, dark green in color and predominantly filamentous, though everywhere that moderately stable mud was available the puffballs and chytrids clustered, climbing upon one another's backs, forming grotesque conglomerates of form and feature, bristling with the ascocarps and the hydroids of two or three dozen different species. The water here was acidic, and it burned their skin, as well as hastening the rot which had already set into Joth's clothes. There were no replacements, and as time passed he grew gradually more naked. Even the spore-free air of the wetlands was no relief to them, because it carried vitriolic vapors which irritated the tissues inflamed by the spores.

They never dared rest in the wetlands, even where the soil was matted into plate-like ridges by the dense algal filaments. They had to share such refuges with a large variety of inimical creatures which, though small, were not negligible. Crabs in particular abounded in such regions.

There were also large plants whose gigantic rubbery leaves lay atop the moist surface, offering a refuge of a kind, but if they stayed on such a leaf for more than a few moments it would begin to sink beneath their weight, and they would be flooded. From time to time, when they walked over such platforms, they would be tipped sideways into the morass, which was more like deep slime than mud.

The wetlands also sheltered flesh-eating plants like soft sea-anemones, with tentacles which never ceased to writhe through the air and through the mud. The plants never stopped consuming victims of one kind or another—they had to keep moving in order to catch prey, and they had to catch prey in order to keep moving.

In the swamps they were occasionally alarmed by the sight of large animals. But the animals were always equally alarmed, and often they would know of the presence of the larger beasts only by the loud splashing of a creature in full retreat.

More dangerous, and on one occasion all but deadly, were the four-foot flatworms which lurked invisibly in the fluid subsurface. One of these wrapped itself around Huldi's ankle and tripped her. She fell full length, but caught herself on her hands, and did not allow her head to go into the mud. The worm flopped up on to her back like a great wet blanket. Huldi tried to shrug it off, but was too firmly imbedded in the mud. Joth grabbed it but couldn't hold it. Its head was between her shoulder blades, and it seemed to spit at her, everting its whole gut. Glands in the gut were churning out digestive juices like bubbling fountains, and the villi of the blind intestine could be seen flapping like a thousand tiny flags.

Joth eventually managed to get a hold as Huldi writhed and screamed, and between them they tossed the creature sideways so that the flood of corrosive liquid was lost in the slime. There was an audible hiss as the acids sank into the algal soup. Huldi was burned about the neck, and had to abandon what was left of her jacket, but she escaped without any serious injury.

Joth stamped hard on the worm, but the ground was so slushy that it came to no real harm. It writhed and sucked its gut back into itself and oozed away into the glutinous subsurface.

Eventually, they came to the edge of a land which seemed to have rusted away. Joth guessed immediately that here were the partially unreclaimed ruins of a city, and he wanted to go into this land in search of relics of an older mankind. But Nita stopped him, saying that it was too dangerous, and that such lands were deadly. She pointed away to the west, and Joth saw a strip of darkness in the further sky. The stars, which were clustered less densely even in the roof directly above, petered out completely in that direction.

"The black land," she said. "Perpetual night."

"Not quite," said Joth, straining his metal eyes, and then adjusting them with his thumb to give him better vision. "I can see a thin line of light, like a road of stars. It goes straight out into the black land. Where does it lead? It can't be there without a reason. It points a way...somewhere."

"No one knows where it goes," said Nita. "We have come far to the west. We are away from our true direction. We must turn away from this country. We must not cross it, and we would die if we tried."

They went on, away from the region where echoes of an older civilization still lingered. On towards the metal wall. They all became tired and sick, and ultimately neither Nita nor Huldi enjoyed any kind of an advantage over Joth, nor the one over the other. Whereas in the early times it had been Nita and Huldi who gathered most of the food, now they all shared equally in the work. They slept in turn, fitfully and uneasily, and they were all troubled in some measure by the quality of their dreams. They questioned neither the purpose of the journey nor the distance which they covered. There was no suggestion, at any time, that Nita might prefer to turn back and search for her father, or that Huldi might want to go her own way. They were united, by a kind of love. And also by a kind of fear (though love itself has always a component of fear, no matter what kind it might be). But their fears were quiet fears, which they neither voiced nor faced.

67.

In the end, they found the metal wall.

68.

Carl Magner went down.
Alone.
Neither Abram Ravelvent, nor Julea, had come into the plexus after him. They had not tried to stop him, though perhaps they might have had they realized what was happening. They did not follow him. Julea had broken down into tears, and simply collapsed like a rag doll, as if it had all been inevitable from the very beginning, and now was finished. Ravelvent had been momentarily torn between them, but there had been no real choice to make. He had stayed with Julea, and with the world that was his, and Magner had gone into the plexus alone, with a

bullet lodged in his body.

Perhaps there was the faintest of possibilities that if it had not been for the bullet Magner would have turned back. But any impetus which he might have lacked the bullet had most certainly provided. It was the final settlement, the *coup de grâce*. It left nothing else for Carl Magner but a descent to the Hell he had named.

There was no more help now. There was no more reality except the world of sleep (perpetual sleep) and dreams (are there dreams in death?).

Carl Magner was running. Down.

He was coming face to face with Heaven and Hell. Running between the worlds, he was their marriage—the only marriage they would ever know.

He went down.

And down.

And down.

Crystal eyes winked at him. Plastic mesh ears caught the sound of his coughing, the rattle of his clattering feet, the slow slap, slap, slap of the tiny drops of blood on the stairs. The blood would have clotted if only he would have let it, but instead he went down, and tore himself apart a fraction farther with every step that he took, tore the corners of the wound again and again, until a tiny rounded bullet hole became an ugly gaping mouth. Blood drooled.

Slap, slap, slap.

Down, and down.

The plexus could feel him as well. It could feel his vibrations, his hurry, his urgency, his need. And his slowly draining life. The plexus was conscious of him. It knew him. Impassively, it crouched around him and watched him, studied his scurrying figure.

He was very tiny.

He was tasteless. The machine could not smell him. It could only see and hear and feel. It had no direct emotional/sensory links. Its organometallic synapses were geared to a functional régime of an altogether different character.

He was not thinking. Not really. He had nothing to think about, nothing to keep his mind active except the simple routine of operating his motor nerves. After the bullet, the future had disappeared. In a puff of smoke. The past was dwindling and fading. In a puff of blood.

The whole consciousness of time and its meaning (past/present/future) which Carl Magner had used to fuel his life recoiled into him like a snapped watchspring. The past was kneeling on the grass up above, Julea in Ravelvent's arms. The future....

He was caged in the present, caged and confined by bars which pressed on his being like the laces of a straightjacket. His meaninglessness meant nothing, here. He was only acting a part as he ran down the staircase to throw wide the door which opened the Underworld.

He hurled himself down, trying to outrun the running of the blood.

And down.

And down.

And down.

69.

When Carl Magner reached the door to the Underworld he found that it was open. All he had to do was push it and it swung out. There was no lock, no apparent catch, and the hinges were not stiff. It required only the effort of his feeble fingers to push it open.

The door opened to reveal the land of his dreams.

There was silence and starlight.

Carl Magner realized that the door had been open for thousands of years.

70.

Joth watched the door in the metal wall swing slowly outwards. They had been walking beside the wall for some miles. Joth did not know how many. He did not know—he literally had no idea—whether it had been three minutes or three hours or three weeks since they had first sighted the wall towering above the Swithering Waste and occluding the far stars.

Nita and Huldi paused, and then stayed still. But after momentary hesitation Joth went on. He did not know what hid behind the door, but he knew that it had come from above, from his own world, and he knew that there could be no reason to be afraid.

By the time Joth reached the door, Carl Magner was stretched out on the damp earth. His face was in the dirt. His feet were still on the steel sill of the final step.

Joth turned him over, and cradled his head in his own lap. Carl Magner's eyes were open, and he was looking up at the still, pearl-white stars. Joth could not be sure that his father could still see.

"Joth?" said Magner. Magner knew that he was not dreaming. There was no Joth in the dreams. There never had been. There never could be. Not even a dream of death could bring Joth into the world of frozen stars. This was reality, of a kind.

"It's me," said Joth. "I was coming back. I found the way. If you'd waited, I would have come. There was no need."

Joth did not know there was a bullet in his father's back. He could feel the slight wetness where his father's spine rested against his thigh, but he assumed that the dampness was in his own clothing. He did not know that his father was on the brink of death, even though he looked down into eyes which stared, and which would soon be quite sightless.

"I came...," said Carl Magner.

"It's all right," said Joth. "You can see. It's all right. Look at the stars. The world is real. The people...only the people...."

"I was wrong," said Magner.

"Yes," said Joth, "you were wrong."

They were talking about two very different kinds of wrongness. But neither of them knew. They thought that they understood.

Then Carl Magner died.

ABOUT THE AUTHOR

Brian Stableford was born in Yorkshire in 1948. He taught at the University of Reading for several years, but is now a full-time writer. He has written many science-fiction and fantasy novels, including *The Empire of Fear, The Werewolves of London, Year Zero, The Curse of the Coral Bride, The Stones of Camelot*, and *Prelude to Eternity*. Collections of his short stories include a long series of *Tales of the Biotech Revolution*, and such idiosyncratic items as *Sheena and Other Gothic Tales* and *The Innsmouth Heritage and Other Sequels*. He has written numerous nonfiction books, including *Scientific Romance in Britain, 1890-1950*; *Glorious Perversity: The Decline and Fall of Literary Decadence*; *Science Fact and Science Fiction: An Encyclopedia*; and *The Devil's Party: A Brief History of Satanic Abuse*. He has contributed hundreds of biographical and critical articles to reference books, and has also translated numerous novels from the French language, including books by Paul Féval, Albert Robida, Maurice Renard, and J. H. Rosny the Elder.

www.ingramcontent.com/pod-product-compliance
Lightning Source LLC
Chambersburg PA
CBHW050744250626
47155CB00005B/1923